POEMS OF THE LATE T'ANG

ADVISORY EDITOR: BETTY RADICE

ANGUS CHARLES GRAHAM was born in 1919. He was Professor of Classical Chinese at the School of Oriental and African Studies, University of London, from 1971 until his retirement in 1984. In 1981 he became a fellow of the British Academy. Among his publications are *Two Chinese Philosophers: Ch'eng Ming-tao and Ch'eng Yi-ch'uan* (1958), *The Book of Lieh Tʒŭ* (1960), *The Problem of Value* (1961), *Poems of the Late T'ang* (1965), *Later Mohist Logic, Ethics and Science* (1978), *Chuang-tʒŭ: The Seven Inner Chapters and Other Writings from the Book of Chuang-tʒŭ* (1981), *Reason and Spontaneity* (1985) and *Yin-Yang and the Nature of Correlative Thinking* (1986). He died in 1991.

POEMS OF
THE LATE T'ANG

Translated with an Introduction by
A. C. GRAHAM

PENGUIN BOOKS

PENGUIN BOOKS

Published by the Penguin Group
Penguin Books Ltd, 27 Wrights Lane, London W8 5TZ, England
Penguin Books USA Inc., 375 Hudson Street, New York, New York 10014, USA
Penguin Books Australia Ltd, Ringwood, Victoria, Australia
Penguin Books Canada Ltd, 10 Alcorn Avenue, Toronto, Ontario, Canada M4V 3B2
Penguin Books (NZ) Ltd, 182–190 Wairau Road, Auckland 10, New Zealand

Penguin Books Ltd, Registered Offices: Harmondsworth, Middlesex, England

This translation first published 1965
Reprinted with additional Preface 1977
10 9 8 7 6

Copyright © A. C. Graham, 1965
All rights reserved

Printed in England by Clays Ltd, St Ives plc
Set in Monotype Fournier

UNESCO COLLECTION OF REPRESENTATIVE WORKS —
CHINESE SERIES

This book has been accepted in the Chinese Translations
Series of the United Nations Educational, Scientific and
Cultural Organization (UNESCO).

For Der Pao

Poetry presents the thing in order to convey the feeling. It should be precise about the thing and reticent about the feeling, for as soon as the mind responds and connects with the thing the feeling shows in the words; this is how poetry enters deeply into us. If the poet presents directly feelings which overwhelm him, and keeps nothing back to linger as an aftertaste, he stirs us superficially; he cannot start the hands and feet involuntarily waving and tapping in time, far less strengthen morality and refine culture, set heaven and earth in motion and call up the spirits!

Wei T'ai (eleventh century)

Contents

Preface

This book owes much to conversations some years ago with James Liu, who introduced me to the poems of Li Shang-yin, to the possibility of applying post-Empsonian critical techniques to late T'ang poetry, and to the origins of the ninth-century manner in the last poems of Tu Fu. For several years I have been worrying everyone within reach who knows Chinese for advice on obscure points and criticisms of my draft versions, among others Dr Waley, Prof. David Hawkes, Jerome Ch'en, Ch'eng Hsi, D. C. Lau, and Mrs Katherine Whittaker. I should like to thank all of them for their patience, and also Douglas Hewitt, the first to give me the reactions of a reader who knows no Chinese.

Earlier drafts of some of these translations have been contributed to *The Review*, No. 9 (1963) and the *Anthology of Chinese Literature* edited by Cyril Birch (Grove Press, forthcoming).

My thanks are also due to Dr Waley and George Allen and Unwin Ltd for permission to quote from Arthur Waley's *Chinese Poems*; *Li Fu-jen* and part of *New Corn*; to Mr Ezra Pound for permission to quote his *Lui Ch'e*; and to the Houghton Mifflin Company for permission to quote *To the air: 'The Fallen Leaves and the Plaintive Cicada'* from Amy Lowell's *Fir Flower Tablets*.

1965   A. C. G.

Additional Preface

In the discussion of the relation between Far Eastern poetry and the beginnings of English modernism on pp. 15–16 I missed an interesting piece of information which has turned up since. I wrote that 'the Japanese influence goes back at least to 1909' (to the Eiffel Tower circle which included T. E. Hulme, F. S. Flint, Edward Storer, and afterwards Pound). Wallace Martin (in J. Howard Woolmer's *Catalogue of the Imagist Poets*, New York, 1966) has since explored the genesis of Imagism in the writings of the Eiffel Tower circle, in particular the *New Age* poetry reviews from 1908 onwards by Flint, who in the issue of 9 December 1909 praises Storer for 'aiming at a form of expression, like the Japanese, in which an image is the resonant heart of an exquisite moment'. These reviews confirm the impression that Flint, in spite of his own proneness to second-hand phrases, was one of the originators of the new approach to poetry, and the first to introduce it to the public. It turns out that his first review on 11 July 1908 (the earliest firmly dated document found by Martin) actually starts with a book of Japanese *tanka* in rhymed translations. He praises it enthusiastically at the expense of other books he is reviewing, objecting only to the traditional versification ('I could have wished that the poems in this book had been translated into little dropping rhythms, unrhymed'); and he quotes two *haikai* in free verse translations to show how the Japanese convey 'the suggestion, not the complete picture'. He proceeds directly to his first call for a new kind of poetry: 'To the poet who can catch and render, like these Japanese, the brief fragments of his soul's music, the future lies open.' He declares that 'the day of the lengthy poem is over – at least for this troubled age', and the poet 'must write, I think, like these Japanese, in snatches of song'.

1977   A. C. G.

The Translation of Chinese Poetry

The art of translating Chinese poetry is a by-product of the Imagist movement, first exhibited in Ezra Pound's *Cathay* (1915), Arthur Waley's *One Hundred and Seventy Chinese Poems* (1918), and Amy Lowell's *Fir Flower Tablets* (1921). Except for Waley, the unique instance of a sinologist who is also a poet, its best practitioners have always been poets or amateurs working on the draft versions of others. Its problems are in some respects peculiar; there is no language which gives a translator less cause to flatter himself that he has achieved a perfect re-creation, yet worthwhile partial successes are unexpectedly easy. Classical Chinese is a language of uninflected and generally monosyllabic words grammatically organized solely by word-order and the placing of particles. Its strength lies in its concreteness and conciseness, grammatical particles being rarer in literary prose than in speech and in verse than in prose. When a Chinese poet writes abstractly it is nearly impossible to make him interesting in English:

K'UANG	HENG	K'ANG	SU	KUNG-MING	PO
K'uang	Heng	write-frankly	memorial.	Success	slight
LIU	HSIANG	CH'UAN	CHING	HSIN-SHIH	WEI
Liu	Hsiang	transmit	classic.	Plan	miss.

This couplet, in which the poet contrasts his own failures with the successes of two ancient statesmen, can hardly be rendered into even tolerable English without considerable rephrasing:

> A disdained K'uang Heng, as a critic of policy.
> As promoter of learning, a Liu Hsiang who failed.

The element in poetry which travels best is of course concrete imagery; however little we may care for Goethe or

Pushkin in English, we react immediately to Lorca, and even feel ourselves qualified to judge whether he is a great poet or merely the manipulator of a firework display. Fortunately, most Chinese poetry is extremely concrete:

HU	CHIAO	YIN	PEI	FENG
Tartar	horn	tug	North	wind,
CHI	MEN	PAI	YÜ	SHUI (rhyme)
Thistle	Gate	white(r)	than	water.
T'IEN	HAN	CH'ING-HAI	TAO	
Sky	hold-in-mouth	Kokonor	road,	
CH'ENG	T'OU	YÜEH	CH'IEN	LI (rhyme)
Wall	top	moon	thousand	mile.

Various lucky accidents make it possible to translate such poetry more literally from Chinese than from Indo-European languages. Chinese and English word-order are similar although not identical. All poets except for a few experimenters confine the sentence within the couplet and generally within the line. Since the English line tends to have as many stresses as there are concrete words in the Chinese it is possible, as Waley was the first to notice, to render almost as literally in sprung verse as in prose. These features partly account for the greater success of poetic translation from Chinese than from Japanese, which has conjugation, a different order of words and of clauses, and sentences running over several lines, so that the translator, forced to proceed in another sequence, finds himself writing a drastically different poem. The English reader of a poem in Chinese constantly discovers that several lines have almost translated themselves, and after such a good start can hardly resist translating the whole:

A Tartar horn tugs at the North wind,
Thistle Gate shines whiter than the stream.
The sky swallows the road to Kokonor:
On the Great Wall, a thousand miles of moonlight.

As these lines illustrate, the ideal of perfect literalness is soon betrayed by concessions to idiomatic smoothness, rhythm, and immediate intelligibility. 'Swallow' is not quite the Chinese *han*. 'Water', unfortunately, clashes in sound with 'whiter', and is replaced by 'stream'. With some misgivings, since the only sacrosanct thing is the image, one strengthens '(is) white(r)' to 'shines whiter', partly to keep the verbal force of the Chinese adjective, which acts like an intransitive verb, and partly to show up the connexion with moonlight in the last line. The 'wall', which the poet did not need to identify, becomes 'the Great Wall'. In spite of the factors which sometimes make translation easier from Chinese than from Latin or French, it is hardly necessary to say that the meanings and associations of Chinese words differ much more from their apparent English equivalents than do words in Indo-European languages. Above all, fidelity to the image is impossible without a complete disregard of the verse forms of the original, some of which are as rigid and elaborate as the sonnet. Almost all Chinese poetry is rhymed, and most classical forms have lines with equal numbers of syllables, so that it is understandable that some translators still prefer to take liberties with the sense in order to impose iambics and rhyme. The sacrifice of strict form for the sake of content was first made possible by the doctrine that the essence of poetry is the Image, the exact presentation of which imposes an absolute rhythm out of accord with regular verse forms. It is this connexion with Imagism which already gives most Chinese translations a little of the period look of Chapman's or Pope's Homer, combining the visual precision, transitive drive, and emotional reticence common to Chinese and early modernist English poetry with a rhythmic freedom and naturalness of diction which belong to the latter alone.

It is well known that glimpses of Japanese and Chinese poetry contributed to the clarification of the Imagist ideal, acting like the Japanese woodcut on Impressionism and African sculpture on Cubism. The Japanese influence goes back at least to 1909, when T. E. Hulme deserted his year-old Poets' Club for a circle of like-minded poets which included F. S. Flint.[1] Flint, who begins his miniature *History of Imagism*[2] with this circle, says that among other possibilities it discussed the replacement of traditional verse forms by 'pure *vers libre*; by the Japanese *tanka* and the *haikai*; we all wrote dozens of the latter as an amusement . . .', and that before joining he had already been advocating 'a poetry in *vers libre*, akin in spirit to the Japanese'. The French vogue for translating and imitating the three-line *haikai* (*hokku*), started by P. L. Couchoud in 1905,[3] was evidently among the Parisian influences active during this formative period. Pound's account in *Vorticism*[4] of the genesis of what he calls his '*hokku*-like sentence' *In a Station of the Metro* in 1912, the year in which he invented the name 'Les Imagistes', shows clearly both the Japanese inspiration of the verse and its importance in his own development. Interest shifted from Japan to China after 1913, when Pound received the manuscripts of Ernest Fenollosa, the American who introduced the classical art of Japan to a Western public previously familiar only with the woodcut. These included the *Essay on the Chinese Written Character*, from which Pound took his misconceptions about ideograms as well as a valuable theory of the key function of the transitive verb in poetic syntax, and the draft versions of Chinese poems[5] which he adapted in *Cathay* (keeping Fenollosa's Japanese transcriptions: his 'Rihaku' is Li Po).

1. Cf. E. R. Miner, *The Japanese Tradition in British and American Literature* (Princeton, 1958). 2. *Egoist*, 1 May 1915.

3. Cf. W. L. Schwarz, *The Imaginative Interpretation of the Far East in Modern French Literature* (Paris, 1927), 159 ff.

4. *Fortnightly*, 1 September 1914.

5. For a specimen, see Lawrence W. Chisolm, *Fenellosa: the Far East and American Culture* (Yale, 1963), 251f.

The syllables of Chinese – in the classical language, generally monosyllabic words – are written with separate characters, of which all contain a 'radical' pointing to the sense and most a 'phonetic' pointing to the sound. Thus the word *sheng* 生 'birth' is the ancestor of *hsing* 性 'human nature', written with the same character as phonetic but differentiated by the 'heart' radical, and of *hsing* 姓 'surname', written similarly with the 'woman' radical. We understand the etymology of the latter words primarily from the characters, without which we should hardly be certain that the phonetic resemblance to *sheng* was more than an accident. Because of this combination of phonetic poverty and graphic wealth the system of meanings and associations touched off by a Chinese word inheres not in its sound structure but in the construction of the character. This fact has suggested to many that Chinese writing enhances the visual quality of poetry, since many characters are still vaguely recognizable as the pictures from which they developed (*k'ou* 口 'mouth', *jih* 日 'sun', *mu* 目 'eye'), and in any case they easily act on the imagination like blobs in the Rorschach test. It is rather difficult to estimate this effect since a habitual reader of Chinese is hardly conscious of it without deliberately analysing his reactions, just as the reader of an English poem may not notice that the spelling of SPHINX, by marking it as a Greek borrowing, has effects which would be damaged by spelling it SFINKS. Certainly, one can give too much weight to the visual aspect of Chinese writing. Poems in China, as elsewhere, are firstly patterns of sound, and many verse forms have begun as song forms; it is untrue, for example, that a poet will choose a word for the appearance of its character in the poem seen as a piece of calligraphy. But it is reasonable to say that the character does exert a sort of visual onomatopoeia, stimulating the eye as the ear is stimulated by 'hubbub', 'whisper', or 'clatter', words which in themselves are no more like the sounds which they imitate than the character for 'sun' is like the sun.

Obviously, there is no way of reproducing this effect short of inventing a similar system of logographic writing for English. But some translators of the 1920s did suppose that it was necessary to take account of the structure of a character by introducing some of its elements into the English version.[1] There is some risk of exaggerating the extent to which this practice vitiated the Imagist translations, for Pound did not adopt it until after publishing *Cathay* and Amy Lowell experimented with it very cautiously (although her collaborator Florence Ayscough later went much farther); Waley, of course, always knew better. The construction of a character is not a simple matter and was often misunderstood. But even where there is no misunderstanding the effect of the practice is to push into the foreground associations which are as far back in the poem as the similar associations of an English word, and to lose by diffuseness effects which are not worth making unless, as in Chinese, they are compressed into a single word. A poem of Li Po begins:

CH'ÜAN	FEI	SHUI	SHENG	CHUNG
Dog	bark	water	sound	middle

A dog barks amid the sound of water.

The character *fei* 吠 'bark' consists of 'dog' with the 'mouth' radical on the left. If there happened to be a common English word the etymology of which suggested a dog opening its mouth, a translator might well pounce on it gratefully; since there is not, he had better be content with 'bark'. But Amy Lowell translated:

1. Apart from Pound, the translator who has resorted most to character-splitting is Florence Ayscough, *Tu Fu; the Autobiography of a Chinese Poet* (London, 1929). For the functions of the Chinese character in poetry, cf. J. Y. Liu, *The Art of Chinese Poetry* (London, 1962), pp. 3–19.

A dog,   A dog barking,
And the sound of rushing water.[1]

The effect is simply to break the syntax of the original and make a pointless repetition. She is also too informative about the sound, although the pressure to take this kind of liberty is so often irresistible that I cannot protest with an entirely easy conscience. The gift of terseness is the least dispensible literary qualification of a translator from Chinese, and the illusion that to work in everything one must go on adding words is the cause of the paradox that some of the sparest Chinese writers seem windbags when read in English.

The culminating period of Chinese poetry is the T'ang dynasty (618–907); its most famous poets are Li Po (701–62) and Tu Fu (712–70). During these three centuries obstacles to the translator steadily multiply – increasing density of language, an allusiveness which often forces him to bury a poem in commentary, elaborate versification which shakes his confidence that the sacrifice of form for content is necessarily a sound bargain. Amateur translators have naturally congregated around the great names, if only because they do not know where else to go; Pound would hardly have settled on Li Po, in Chinese terms a decidedly romantic poet, if he had had much to choose from. Waley at first disliked most T'ang poetry, as he shows in the preface to *One Hundred and Seventy Chinese Poems*. Even after he began to like it better he preferred to confine himself to the poetry which loses least in English, to the pre-T'ang poets and to Po Chü-i (772–846), who reverted to a simpler style. But there is a strong reason for making an attempt on poets even later than Li Po and Tu Fu, in spite of the small hope of conveying more than a diminishing fraction of their achievement. This is the increasing complexity of language and imagination which makes them much the most interesting of Chinese poets to a reader whose tastes have been guided by

1. *Fir Flower Tablets*, 68.

William Empson rather than by Hulme or Pound. Apart from a scatter of anthology items and the pieces by Li Ho in the *Poems of Solitude* of Michael Bullock and Jerome Ch'en, they are still unknown except to sinologists. The English reader continues to recognize Chinese poetry by the face which it turned towards the poetic revolutionaries of the second decade of the century, just as he knows Persian poets only as world-weary wine-bibbing Victorian aesthetes. If it should occur to him to ask, for example, why all Chinese poetry has such a sharp definition, without any of the shadow and mystery which he senses in Sung landscape painting or Taoist philosophy, the answer is that this is the quality in poetry which least interested poets at the crucial moment of the revolt against Romanticism.

The emergence of this new sensibility seems to be quite a sudden event in the history of a literature. Although closer inspection might reveal a more gradual process, one has the impression that Japanese poetry begins to concentrate multiple meanings during the ninth century, English in the late sixteenth, French as recently as the nineteenth; in China it is plausible to trace the beginnings of the development to the poems which Tu Fu wrote after his arrival in K'uei-chou in 766.[1] An example is this couplet from the first poem in his cycle *Autumn Meditation*:

TS'UNG	CHÜ	LIANG	K'AI	/	T'O	JIH	LEI
KU	CHOU	I	HSI	/	KU	YÜAN	HSIN

Subject				Adjectival phrase		
Adjective	Noun	Adverb		Verb	Adjective	Noun	Noun
Cluster	chrysanthemum	two		open /	other	day	tear,
Lonely	boat		one (wholly)	tie /	former	garden	heart

1. Kurokawa Yoichi has also traced the beginnings of poetic ambiguity in Chinese to Tu Fu's K'uei-chou poems, and has examined in detail the same couplet from *Autumn Meditation*: 'An Introduction to Tu Fu's "Eight Autumn Poems"' (in Japanese), *Journal of Chinese Literature* (Kyoto University), April 1956.

The syntax of the two parts of each line is plain, and reinforced by the grammatical parallelism of the lines; yet one is left suspended between two possibilities, that the sentences end at the caesura or that they continue to the end of the line:

> The clustered chrysanthemums have twice opened. Another day's tears.
> The lonely boat is tied once and for all. Thoughts of my 'former garden' [cliché for 'home'],

or

> The clustered chrysanthemums have twice released another day's tears,
> The lonely boat wholly ties the thoughts of my former garden.

Amy Lowell chose the first alternative:

> The myriad chrysanthemums have bloomed twice. Days to come——tears.
> The solitary little boat is moored, but my heart is in the old-time garden.[1]

William Hung prefers the second:

> The sight of chrysanthemums again loosens the tears of past memories;
> To a lonely detained boat I vainly attach my hope of going home.[2]

Neither of the translators can be convicted of saying anything not implicit in the original; they differ so widely because the English language imposes choices which the poet refrained from making. Is it the flowers which burst open or the tears, the boat which is tied up or the poet's heart? Is the 'other day' past, or a future day which may be as sad

1. *ut sup.* 113.
2. *Tu Fu: China's Greatest Poet* (Cambridge, Mass., 1952), p. 233.

as the two autumns in which he has already seen the chrysan-
themums open in this unfamiliar country? Are the tears his
own, or the dew on the flowers? Were they, or will they be,
shed on another day, or is he shedding them now for the
sorrows of another day? Are his hopes wholly tied to the
boat which may take him home, or tied down once for all
by the boat which will never sail? Is his heart tied here with
the boat, or has it travelled home in his imagination to see
other chrysanthemums in his former garden? Most of these
interpretations have been proposed by commentators and
the ideal translation would allow all of them; this is the kind
of language which does mean all that it can mean. A minor
but recurrent problem of translation is illustrated by the
phrase 'former garden' (home). Used in the same couplet
with 'chrysanthemum' the cliché is not quite dead, but Amy
Lowell's literal rendering seems to push the image of the
garden too far into the foreground. My own version eludes
some of these choices but not others:

> The clustered chrysanthemums have opened twice, in tears
> of other days:
> The forlorn boat, once and for all, tethers my homeward
> thoughts.

I am tempted to write '. . . tears of another day'. But
that would be ambiguous in the wrong way, suggesting
either a past day or today; the day should be either past or
future.

Late T'ang poetry, which explores the Chinese language
to the limit of its resources, can be damaged severely by the
irrelevant precisions imposed by Indo-European person,
number, and tense. An example which applies even to older
poetry is the use of pronouns. A Chinese poet seldom writes
'I' unless he is himself an agent in the situation (for example,
Lu T'ung in the *Eclipse*), so that his emotions assume an
impersonality difficult to achieve in English. In some of Li

Shang-yin's poems about women it is an unanswerable – and immaterial – question whether one should supply 'I' (seeing from her point of view) or 'she' (seeing from the poet's). The word 'I', supplied merely because English grammar requires a subject for the verb, can tip a whole poem over on to the side of self-righteousness or self-pity. Tense, and the temporal adjustment of clauses, give frequent trouble in translating Li Ho, a poet obsessed by the passage of time. The following lines are from his *Watchman's Drum*:

> The willows of the Han capital shine yellow on the new
> blinds,
> Flying Swallow's scented bones lie buried in the cypress
> mound:
> It has pounded to pieces a thousand years of suns for ever
> white
> Unheard by the King of Ch'in and Emperor Wu.
> Your hair glints blue, is the colour of the blossoms on the
> reeds. . . .

Although there are no temporal particles in the original, even in the third line, I had written in an earlier draft

> The willows of the Han capital shone yellow on the new
> blinds
> When Flying Swallow's scented bones were buried in the
> cypress mound:
> It has pounded to pieces a thousand years of suns for ever
> white
> Unheard by the King of Ch'in and Emperor Wu.
> Your hair that glinted blue is the colour of the blossoms on
> the reeds. . . .

The revision recovers some of the immediacy of the Chinese, although it exposes the reader to the danger of taking the reed blossoms to be blue instead of white. But either choice disintegrates a vision which fuses past and present. (The T'ang dynasty had returned to the Han capital, Ch'ang-an in the north-west.)

A possible method of retaining Chinese ambiguities would be to prune the translation to a kind of literary pidgin English. The most successful of all English translations, the Bible, deliberately semitized English, beginning sentences with 'And . . .' rather than omit a Hebrew particle; why not do something similar with Chinese? The possibility is especially inviting since the modernist poetry of the 1920s, impatient of the logical connectives which thwart the achievement of a language of pure sensation, did move towards a kind of Sino-English. Several translators have made experiments in this direction, for example, Waley's version of Wu-ti's *Autumn Wind*. For more than one reason, I have made none myself which deserve printing. A strictly word-for-word translation, as several examples in this introduction demonstrate, disrupts English syntax without teaching the reader the syntax of the Chinese; it also requires, to be intelligible at all, a near-perfect equivalent of every word, since it allows no opportunity to compensate for deviations by the phrasing of the sentence. A version in pidgin capable of standing on its own might therefore have to take more liberties with the original than would be necessary in standard English. It is possible, however, that more can be done with this technique than has yet been achieved, perhaps combining it with the part-rhymes to which the English ear has grown accustomed since Wilfred Owen's experiments in dissonance. The awkward but original translations of Wong Man are suggestive in this connexion; some of them sound more like Chinese poems than anything else in English:

> Grass rustle through dim woods,
> Warrior shoots into night,
> Dawn finds arrow-plume
> Lost in rocky heights.

Black moon geese fly high,
Tartars flee the dark;
Light horses pursue,
Sword and bow snow-marked.[1]

However, these are less literal than standard English versions can be, and also involve some over-simplification:

WOOD	DARK	GRASS	STARTLE	WIND
GENERAL		NIGHT	DRAW	BOW
DAWN		SEEK	WHITE	FEATHER
LOST	IN	STONE	CORNER	MIDDLE

Woods dim, grass startled by the wind:
In the night the general draws his bow.
At dawn they seek the white feather
Lost among the corners of the stones.

MOON	BLACK	GOOSE	FLY	HIGH
	KHAN	NIGHT	FLEE	
ABOUT-TO	LEAD	LIGHT	RIDER	PURSUE
GREAT	SNOW	FILL	BOW	SWORD

Moon black, geese fly high:
The Khan flees in the night.
As they lead out the light horse in pursuit
Heavy snow covers bow and sword.

('GENERAL', 'DAWN', 'KHAN', and 'FLEE' are two-syllable words.)

Chinese prosody changed radically more than once in its history. The earliest poetry is generally supposed to be purely syllabic; but down to the last century B.C. one constantly notices irregularities in the length of line and placing of the rhyme, and regularities in the placing of grammatical particles, which suggest the working of another principle,

1. Wong Man, *Poems from China* (*Hsiang-kang ku-chi pien-i she*, Hongkong, no date), p. 29.
The quatrains translated, by Lu Lun (748–800?), are among the *yüeh-fu* in the *Three Hundred T'ang Poems*.

perhaps of stress. For the next six centuries prosody was certainly syllabic, with equal lines of five and later seven syllables. These measures have survived to the present under the name of 'Old Style'; but from the seventh century they were challenged by the 'New Style' versification based on the four tones of Chinese syllables.[1] Most of the poems by Tu Fu, Tu Mu, and Li Shang-yin in this volume are in the New Style, which sometimes betrays itself even in translation by a rigid parallelism of lines within the couplet.

In at least the two middle couplets of the eight-line verse the paired lines are syntactically parallel, and each word contrasts in sense with its counterpart in the other line. Thus in the couplet by Tu Fu quoted earlier,[2] the contrast between CLUSTER and LONELY enhances the impression of the rich abundance of the flowers and the forlornness of the single tiny boat, and even the contrast of TWO and ONE, which may seem artificial since ONE used adverbially has the sense of 'wholly', sharpens the sense of change from one year to the next and of the changelessness of the poet's longing for home and despair of returning. The parallelism syste-

---

1. The New Style patterns class together the three deflected tones (/) in contrast with the level tone (–). Although generally presented separately in a way which hides their symmetry, the patterns can be reduced to a single basic formula:

1	2	3	4	5	6	7
(License)	A	(License)	B	–	A	/
	B		A	/	B	– (rhyme)
	B		A	–	B	/
	A		B	/	A	– (rhyme)

The formula assumes two forms according to whether A is level or deflected; it is doubled to make the eight-line verse; it is fitted to the five-syllable line by cutting off the first two syllables. The first line may also be rhymed, requiring an adjustment of the tones of the last syllables from – A / to / A –. Cf. G. B. Downer and A. C. Graham, 'Tone Patterns in Chinese Poetry', *Bulletin of the School of Oriental and African Studies* (London) 26/1 (1963).

2. Cf. pp. 20–22 above.

matized in the New Style is also among the ordinary resources of the Old Style and of prose. It is clear that in English strict parallelism without the repetition of a word is nearly impossible, while parallelism involving repetition will quickly seem rigid and monotonous. But it is necessary to keep some sense of the constant play of comparison and contrast which is the frame of the poem's imaginative structure. The New Style can hardly tolerate the similes which abound in some Old Style verse of the period; the word 'like', although not always avoided, can give the sensation of a yawning gap in the dense pattern of interacting concrete words. Tu Fu seeing the clearness of the water after a fall of rain does not say 'It is as white as the Milky Way' but

> The River of Heaven white from eternity,
> The Yangtse's shallows limpid since just now.

A further problem is the increasing allusiveness of T'ang poetry.[1] Commentators illustrate nearly every line with quotations from older sources – standard references for mythological, historical, and geographical information, earlier examples of idioms, earlier uses of images which have accumulated special associations. Although this habit of quoting sources verbatim may give a different impression, literary allusion in the narrow sense, unintelligible without reference to a particular text, is not very common even in the latest T'ang poetry, and is as often to a folksong as to a classic. I have provided a complete set of background quotations for one of the most allusive of all Chinese poems, Li Shang-yin's *Patterned Lute*; but various commentators take most of the information from various sources, and many reject the single literary allusion, which is to an aphorism on poetry by a writer of the previous century. Apart from this material, a European needs much information that a Chinese

---

1. Cf. Liu, *ut sup.* pp. 131–45.

takes for granted – that jade used as an epithet is not 'jade-coloured' but white jade (jade dew, snow, moon, hands), that comparisons with eyebrows often assume the custom of painting women's eyebrows green, that the fabulous bird of good omen the *feng*, conventionally translated 'phoenix', has no myth of resurrection, that dragons are generally beneficent creatures which it is customary to imagine at the bottom of any river or pool, that cypresses *do* suggest grave-yards as in the West. The seasons are the quarters of the lunar year, so that in the third month the poet laments that spring is nearly over and in the seventh that autumn has already come. Autumn is the season not of 'mists and mellow fruitfulness' but of high clear skies and transparent waters, and is indicated by signs which we may miss – the hum of cicadas, the wind shedding the leaves of the *wu-t'ung* (a tree with a straight, green trunk, the only one on which the phoenix will perch), the sound of clothes laundered for the cold weather being pounded on the washing-blocks, chrysanthemums, by wilting but scarcely ever by yellow leaves.

How much of this information can a reader be expected to tolerate? Equally important, how much of it will really do him any good? There is more literary allusion in early twentieth-century English than in T'ang poetry; we can read Eliot with excitement although missing most of his references, and when we look one up often find that it en-riches the response disappointingly little. It may seem obvious that a reader of the first couplet quoted in this intro-duction[1] needs to be told that K'uang Heng wrote memorials criticizing policy for which he was promoted by the Emperor Yüan of Han (48–33 B.C.), who was worried by the ill omens of an eclipse and an earthquake; and that Liu Hsiang (79–8 B.C.) collected and edited ancient books for the

1. Cf. p. 13 above.

Imperial library, the first great Chinese bibliographer. Yet no amount of information about their lives adds anything relevant to the fact which is already obvious from the context, that they were a statesman and a scholar whose achievements the poet contrasts with his own failure. In any case, this is a couplet which cannot be made very impressive in English, and it might be better tactics to hurry the reader past it rather than delay him with a note.

There is also the fact that to explain an allusion is not necessarily sufficient to make it function in a poem. Li Shang-yin has the line:

> The fan's sliced moon could not hide her shame.

A Chinese has only to read as far as 'moon' to have the impression of a deserted woman; he is used to fans compared with the moon, which go back to the poem of Lady Pan, abandoned concubine of the Emperor Ch'eng of Han (32–7 B.C.), in which she likened herself to a fan discarded in autumn, of white silk.

> Sliced to make a fan for joyful unions,
> Round, round, like the full moon.

Even if it were possible to bring out all such associations line by line, it requires more than an abstract explanation to make them active; one needs the half-conscious recollection of having met the image before. (Not impossible, by the way, in English; Pound's *Fan-piece for her Imperial Lord* is a variation on Lady Pan's poem.) It might be useful to make an anthology of Chinese translations juxtaposing poems of different periods which use the same images, so that Li Shang-yin's poem would come soon after Lady Pan's; but in a selection made on the present basis it is generally best to ignore such allusions unless they recur. There are other kinds of allusion which are virtually compressed idioms, and these a translator has the right to unpack, as in Tu Mu's

CH'U   WAIST   GUT   SEVER   PALM   MIDDLE   LIGHT

'(Girls with) Ch'u waists broke my heart ("sever the guts", although it would be tempting to translate literally, is a dead metaphor), were light in my palm.'

Rather than explain that King Ling of Ch'u had a weakness for slim waists, and that Lady Pan's rival Flying Swallow was so light that she could dance on a man's palm, it is simpler to translate:

> Slim waists of Ch'u broke my heart, light bodies danced into my palm.

The present translation is annotated in a way which may seem strangely inconsistent; I have analysed several poems in detail, appended a full prose paraphrase to one, loaded many with footnotes or with quotations stuck at the head of the poem, passed over some of the most difficult without a comment. These last, mostly by Li Shang-yin, are poems which are obscure in the original but with imagery so powerful that it may well keep some of its force in English; the reader can take them or leave them as he pleases. The extreme example is Li Shang-yin's sequence *The Walls of Emerald*, which may have been fully intelligible in the ninth century, but now survives only by its hallucinatory qualities, as a sort of Chinese *Kubla Khan*. There is consequently little point in noting even the identifiable allusions, still less in passing on the four explanations of the 'crystal dish' recorded in the edition of Takahashi Kazumi.

The fact that much in a poem of Li Ho or Li Shang-yin inevitably disappears in English by no means implies that it is less suitable for translation than a straightforward poem by T'ao Ch'ien or Po Chü-i. Every translation involves both loss and distortion, and the little which is sacrificed in a simple poem may be the little which makes it a poem. It required Waley's talent and special affinity to render Po Chü-i's verse without turning it into the flattest prose; on the other hand, the imagery of Li Shang-yin's love poetry, however subtly it may be coloured by allusions, however intricately involved in verse patterns, and however variously interpreted by commentators, has an intense, invulnerable life of its own, springing from a theme which touches us intimately in a way that most Chinese themes do not, and it can sometimes blaze with almost the same incandescence in English as in Chinese.

There is also one important compensation for the difficulties of late T'ang poetry: increasing complexity of imagery makes it easier for the individuality of a poet to show through in English. An exasperating feature of translation is the manner in which the translator's personal style is bound to obliterate much of the diversity of the material he works on. Both Pound and Waley have dealt with poems by T'ao Ch'ien (To-em-mei, 365–427) and Li Po (Rihaku, 701–62). Who wrote this?

> Swiftly the years, beyond recall.
> Solemn the stillness of this fair morning.
> I will clothe myself in spring-clothing
> And visit the slopes of the Eastern Hill. . . .

It is a safe guess that many readers unfamiliar with the lines will immediately identify them as Waley's[1] rather than Pound's; but who could identify them as T'ao Ch'ien's? (A few will no doubt *remember* that they are T'ao Ch'ien's.) The whole compass of a varied poetic tradition through fifteen hundred years shrinks in Pound's *Cathay* to less than the difference between his *Altaforte* and his *Hugh Selwyn Mauberley*. A reader may well ask how much that seems to distinguish late T'ang from earlier poetry is the effect of my

1. 'New Corn', in *Chinese Poems* (London, 1961), p. 94.

own style. Unfortunately, he will never get a full answer to that question without learning Chinese, although he may find clues in my versions of some of the poems least typical of the period, such as Han Yü's *Evening* or the simpler poems of Tu Fu and Meng Chiao. However, each of the major poets of the late T'ang has his own pattern of imagery, and I have tried to supply enough of each for the pattern to assert itself. If the reader feels that Tu Fu, Li Ho, and Li Shang-yin sound very much alike, I shall have failed at a point where I should have succeeded. The whole of Chinese civilization looks uniform and stationary from the far-off standpoint of a European who knows it only by a few translations and art books; it would be a pity to miss any opportunity of correcting this illusion of perspective.

There remains one dilemma common to all poetic translation. Beyond a certain point one cannot reconcile the demands of translation and of poetry, and must opt for one or the other. Partial reconciliation is possible because at least one element in poetry, imagery, can function effectively in another language. But however much the imagery may vitalize the rhythm and diction of the English, it is still true that the translator is trying to force into one language an imaginative process natural to another. The result may, and ought to be, poetry – we shall not argue over definitions – but it will not give the final satisfaction of making its impression by the perfect, the only adequate, arrangement of words. For example, New Style parallelism is an artificial manner of developing an idea in English; one may soften it, but cannot abolish it without ceasing to be a translator. Every poetic translator must therefore decide whether to stop at the point from which the English reader will have his best view of Omar Khayyam, or attempt the further step by which Edward Fitzgerald takes his place in the line of English poets.

It follows that the rare versions of foreign poems which

achieve the status of absolute poetry in English will be ones from which we can learn nothing dependable about the originals. This is not because they necessarily belong to the class of free variations, of which Carolyn Kizer's *The Meandering River Poems*[1] inspired by Tu Fu are recent and exquisite examples. It may be simply that the reproducible substance is too thin to weigh down the translator when he begins to soar on the rhythms of his own English. Waley has at least one example, his *New Corn*. This is on a different and higher level of poetry from his other versions of T'ao Ch'ien, and is the only one which shares nothing with the original except its thread of prose sense. (Of course I am not suggesting that one should be ungrateful for such a gift of the gods.) It is remarkable that the poets Pound and Amy Lowell, perhaps because of the special interests of Imagism, generally chose like Waley (and myself) to be translators rather than 'imitators' in the sense of the *Imitations* of Robert Lowell. This choice incidentally involves exposing all their mistakes to outside inspection, and they deserve more credit for this than blame for the mistakes.[2] Even sinologists cannot yet avoid errors detectable by a classically trained Chinese; in any case, since the translation of a poem is either a poem of sorts or nothing, a meticulous academic version may be a mistake from the first line to the last.

Although Pound's *Cathay* implicitly recognizes the poetic ceiling above which one cannot rise without ceasing to be a translator, his *Liu Ch'e* has the inevitability of a fully achieved poem, and he rightly classed it among his original compositions. It is a free variation on H. A. Giles' rhymed version of a lament for a dead concubine by the Emperor Wu of Han (Liu Ch'e, 140–87 B.C.), which later attracted both

1. *Kenyon Review* 25/3 (1963).
2. For a comparison of Pound's versions with the originals, cf. Achilles Fang, 'Fenollosa and Pound', *Harvard Journal of Asiatic Studies*, 20 (1957).

Waley and Amy Lowell. The original is in an ancient song form which allowed free use of grammatical particles, some of which may have been unstressed.[1] It may be useful to compare the four versions.

LO		MEI	HSI	WU	SHENG (rhyme)
Silk		sleeve	ah!,	no	sound.
YÜ		CH'IH	HSI	CH'EN	SHENG (rhyme)
Jade		courtyard	ah!	dust	grow.
HSÜ		FANG	LENG	ERH	CHI-MO
Empty		room	cold	and	still/silent/lonely,
LO	YEH	I	YÜ	CH'UNG	CHIUNG (rhyme)
Fallen	leaf	lean	on	doubled	door-bar.
WANG	PI	MEI	CHIH	NÜ	HSI AN TE
Peer-after	that	beautiful	(particle)	woman	ah!, where find?
KAN	YÜ	HSIN	CHIH	WEI	NING (rhyme)
Feel	my	heart	(particle)	not-yet	at-ease

(Some begin the last line with *an te* taken as a rhetorical 'How can ... ?': 'How can she feel my heart's unrest?')

Gone

The sound of rustling silk is stilled,
With dust the marble courtyard filled.
No footfalls echo on the floor,
Fallen leaves in heaps block up the door. . . .
For she, my pride, my lovely one is lost,
And I am left, in hopeless anguish tossed.

H. A. Giles[2]

Liu Ch'e

The rustling of the silk is discontinued,
Dust drifts over the courtyard,
There is no sound of foot-fall, and the leaves

1. There are reasons for suspecting uncounted syllables, presumably unstressed, in much poetry down to the last century B.C. Cf. A. C. Graham, *The Prosody of the sao poetry in the Ch'u tz'ü, Asia Major* (New Series), 10/2 (1964).

2. *A History of Chinese Literature* (London, 1901), p. 100.

Scurry into heaps and lie still,
And she the rejoicer of the heart is beneath them:

A wet leaf that clings to the threshold.

Ezra Pound[1]

Li Fu-jen

The sound of her silk skirt has stopped.
On the marble pavement dust grows.
Her empty room is cold and still.
Fallen leaves are piled against the doors.
    Longing for that lovely lady
How can I bring my aching heart to rest?

Arthur Waley[2]

To the air: 'The Fallen Leaves and the Plaintive Cicada'

There is no rustle of silken sleeves,
Dust gathers in the Jade Courtyard.
The empty houses are cold, still, without sound.
The leaves fall and lie upon the bars of doorway after doorway.
I long for the Most Beautiful One; how can I attain my desire?
Pain bursts my heart. There is no peace.

Amy Lowell[3]

Giles and Waley translated at first hand, Amy Lowell
from the text as explained to her character by character by
Florence Ayscough. As this selection illustrates, Amy
Lowell's versions are less effective poetry than those of
Pound and Waley, but they are remarkably literal; besides
keeping the original title, she is the only one to cope with the
'doubled' or 'repeated' door-bars of the fourth line (although
the phrase suggests several bars on a door rather than several
barred doors). All the translators succeed in evoking essen-
tially the same scene and mood in the first four lines; even

1. *Personae* (London, 1952), p. 118.
2. *ut sup.* p. 38.
3. *ut sup.* p. 139.

Giles preserves, disfigured by his rhyme and iambics, something which Pound had the insight to discern and recover. But the concreteness of the scene dissolves after the fourth line, and the straightforward sentiment of the last couplet, not to mention its doubtful punctuation, makes it suddenly difficult to round the verse off. Both Giles and Amy Lowell are brought to their knees; Waley flags only a little, but departs considerably from the sense of the concluding line. Pound emerges triumphantly by discarding Giles and writing a new conclusion of his own. His multiple comparison of the dead woman with 'a wet leaf that clings to the threshold' is an example, as Miner notices,[1] of the 'super-posed image' which Pound admired in the Japanese *hokku*. It is Far Eastern in manner and feeling, but it transforms the poem and fully entitles him to claim it for his own.

The present selection omits two important poets of the period, Waley's favourite Po Chü-i, and Han-shan ('Cold Mountain'), who has recently attracted no less than four translators.[2] Po Chü-i was a conscious reactionary against the late T'ang manner; the Han-shan poems, a collection of mysterious origin which began to circulate towards the end of the ninth century, are so far outside the main stream that it is still not quite settled that they belong to the ninth century rather than the eighth or seventh. Fortunately, neither poet has much relevance to the guiding principle of this anthology, which is to trace the course of development in simile and metaphor. (One firm rule of translation has been to use comparison words such as 'like' whenever and only when there are such words in the original.) The main course followed is the advance in metaphorical concentra-

1. *ut sup.* p. 116 f.
2. Waley, *ut sup.* pp. 105–11. Gary Snyder, *Evergreen Review* 2, 6 (1958); Burton Watson, *Cold Mountain: a hundred Poems by the T'ang poet Han-shan* (New York, 1962); Wu Chi-yu, 'A Study of Han-shan', *T'oung-Pao* (Leyden) 45, pp. 392–450 (1957).

tion from the poems of Tu Fu's old age to its climax in Li Shang-yin; the less successful divagation towards simile and a poetry of fancy in Han Yü and Lu T'ung has also received some space. Although there are other considerable poets of the period, some no doubt equals of Han Yü and better than Lu T'ung, those chosen have reasonable claims to be the ones who most extended the possibilities of the poetic language. But in the choice of individual poems I have followed my own taste without sticking too closely to the theme.

Although most of the material in the notes comes from standard Chinese and Japanese commentaries, the occasional post-Empsonian explorations of multiple meanings have no such authority. In China, as in England before Empson provided the tools of analysis, there is often a strong feeling that a line of poetry is impoverished by too precise a prose explanation, and a willingness to allow different readers to see different things in it, but only a vague and fitful awareness that apparently contradictory explanations may all be valid. (The Japanese have been more conscious of ambiguity in their poetry, because of their free use of paronomasia, rare in Chinese.) There are obvious dangers in playing at close criticism in a language and literature not one's own; it would be safer to leave such inquiries to the few Chinese, notably James Liu, whom Western critical techniques have awakened to this aspect of their poetry. However, it is rather less presumptuous to analyse a poem than to translate it; and we can hardly leave translation to the Chinese, since there are few exceptions to the rule that translation is best done into, not out of, one's own language. The analyses are of meanings which I suppose to be in both the original and my own version. I do not mention what I have failed to translate. The reader can know Li Ho or Li Shang-yin only by the English poem, or attempt at a poem; no additional information will bring him any nearer to the poetry of the original.

Late Poems of Tu Fu (712–70)

There is a firm consensus that Tu Fu is the greatest of
Chinese poets; if the Chinese often prefer to speak of their
two greatest poets, the sober Tu Fu and his romantic con-
temporary Li Po, it is no doubt because of a tendency to
think in contrasting pairs which shows itself at every level
from the active male bright Yang and passive female dark
Yin of cosmology down to the parallelism of verse and
prose. He has been copiously translated by Florence Ays-
cough (the most advanced sufferer from the character-
splitting fallacy), William Hung, and Rewi Alley, not to
mention the many anthologists.[1] But it is notable that the
two poetic translators of the first rank, Pound and Waley,
have left him alone, the former perhaps because of his
absence from the material left by Fenollosa, but the latter
certainly by choice. I share some of this reluctance: for Tu
Fu presents many of the difficulties to translation of Li Ho
and Li Shang-yin, but lacks the charged themes of death and
love and the strongly personal imagery which establish the
latter as vividly individual poets. The mere fact that he is
the greatest, the most representative figure of the T'ang tends
to make him sound in English like anyone's idea of a
Chinese poet.

Fortunately, the special interests of this selection excuse
me from the duty of conveying Tu Fu's full range. The
pieces chosen are all from the last four years of his life, and
illustrate the beginnings of some of the tendencies which
transformed the poetic language in the ninth century. The

1. Florence Ayscough, *Tu Fu: the Autobiography of a Chinese Poet*
(London, 1929).

William Hung, *Tu Fu: China's Greatest Poet* (Cambridge, Mass.,
1952).

Rewi Alley, *Tu Fu: Selected Poems* (Peking, 1962).

climax both of T'ang poetry and of the power of the dynasty was the reign of Ming-huang (713–55); from 755 the rebellion of An Lu-shan permanently weakened the dynasty and scattered the poets to the ends of China. Tu Fu left the capital Ch'ang-an in the north west in 758, and arrived in 766 at K'uei-chou on the middle Yangtse. During his two years at K'uei-chou he wrote the most famous of his last poems, in which the bitterness of exile and failure in a ruined Empire is lightened by glimpses of a hard-won serenity. In 770 he died soon after leaving Ch'ang-sha, south of the Yangtse, on a journey back to the capital.

The Autumn Wastes

1

The autumn wastes are each day wilder:
Cold in the river the blue sky stirs.
I have tied my boat to the Well Rope Star of barbarians,
Sited my house in a village of Ch'u.
Though the dates are ripe let others cut them down,
I'll hoe for myself where the mallows run to seed.
From the old man's dinner on my plate
I'll scatter my alms to the fish in the brook.

2

Easy to sense the trend in the drift of life,
Hard to compel one creature out of its course.
In the deepest water is the fish's utmost joy,
In the leafiest wood the bird will find its home.
Age and decline are content to be poor and sick,
Praise and blame belong to youth and glory.
Though the autumn wind blows on my staff and pillow
I shall not weary of the North Mountain's ferns.

3

Music and rites to conquer my failings,
Mountains and woods to prolong my zest.
On my twitching head the silk cap slants,
I sun my back in the shine of bamboo books,
Pick up the pine cones dropped by the wind,
Split open the hive when the sky is cold
By scattered and tiny red and blue
Halt pattened feet close to the faint perfume.

4

The autumn sands are white on the far shore,
The glow of evening reddens the mountain range.
Submerged scales push startled ripples,
Returning wings veer with the high wind.
The pounding of washing blocks echoes from house to
    house,
Woodcutters' voices sing the same tune.
The frost flies down in the care of the Dark Maid,
But the blanket she gives parts me from the Southern
    Palace.

5

My ambition, to be pictured in Unicorn Hall:
But my years decline where the ducks and herons troop.
On the great river autumn is soon in spate,
In the empty gorge the night is full of noises.
The by-paths hide in a thousand piling stones:
The sail has come to a stop, one streak of cloud.
My children too have learned a barbarous tongue,
Though it's not so sure they will rise to high command.

Verse 1, lines 3, 4. The poem was written in 767 at K'uei-chou, in
ancient times part of the half-barbarous kingdom of Ch'u. Tu Fu often
compares himself, as in *At the Corner of the World* and *Deep in Winter*,
with the Ch'u poet Ch'ü Yüan (c. 300 B.C.), who was slandered at
court, went into exile, and died by throwing himself into Mi-lo river.
Astrologically the region centred on Mount Min, the destiny of which
depended on the Well Rope Star.
    Verse 4, lines 7, 8. The Dark Maid (cf. Li Shang-yin's *Frosty Moon*)
is the goddess who sends down the frost and snow. The Southern
Palace is a constellation, the name of which was also given to one of the
ministries, the *shang-shu sheng*. At night the poet thinks nostalgically
of his time of glory at the capital; the blanket of frost suggests the
coverlet issued for night duty at the ministry.

Verse 5, lines 1, 2. Unicorn Hall was decorated with pictures of eleven great ministers. Tu Fu, who never rose to be a minister, has ended among the 'ducks and snowy herons', a cliché for the rank-and-file court officials (here also a literal reference to the river birds?).

Verse 5, lines 7, 8. Ho Lung, an earlier official in the same region, frivolously wrote a foreign word into his verse at a poetry competition, excusing himself on the ground that he had lived too long among barbarians.

At the Corner of the World

By Yangtse and Han the mountains pile their barriers.
A cloud in the wind, at the corner of the world.
Year in, year out, there's no familiar thing,
And stop after stop is the end of my road.
In ruin and discord, the Prince of Ch'in-ch'uan:
Pining in exile, the courtier of Ch'u.
My heart in peaceful times had cracked already,
And I walk a road each day more desolate.

Midnight

By the West Pavilion, on a thousand feet of cliff,
Walking at midnight under my latticed window.
Flying stars pass white along the water,
Transparent beams of moonset flicker on the sand.
At home in its tree, notice the secret bird:
Safe beneath the waves, imagine the great fishes.
From kinsmen and friends at the bounds of heaven and
    earth
Between weapon and buffcoat seldom a letter comes.

Stars and Moon on the Yangtse

After sudden rain, a clear autumn night.
On golden waves the sparkle of the Jewelled Cord.
The River of Heaven white from eternity,
The Yangtse's shallows limpid since just now.
Reflections, pearls from a snapped string:
High in the sky one mirror rises.
Afterlight which fades as the clock drips,
Still fainter as the dewdrops settle on the flowers.

To My Younger Brother
(One of a pair)

To my fifth younger brother Feng, living alone in Chiangnan, of whom there has been no news for nearly four years, I send these poems if I can find a messenger.

Rumours that you lodge in a mountain temple
In Hang-chou, or in Yüeh-chou for sure.
Wind in the dust prolongs our day of parting,
Yangtse and Han have wasted my clear autumn.
My shadow sticks to the trees where gibbons scream,
But my spirit whirls by the towers sea-serpents breathe.
Let me go down next year with the spring waters
And search for you to the end of the white clouds in the
    East.

Tu Fu is high up the Yangtse in the gibbon-haunted K'uei-chou region; he imagines his brother near the mouth, within sight of the water-spouts and sea-mirages.
   'Wind in the dust': the turmoil of war which separates them (and the dust of his wheels as he drove away lingering in Tu Fu's memory?).

Yangtse and Han

By Yangtse and Han, a stranger who thinks of home,
One withered pedant between the Ch'ien and K'un.
Under as far a sky as that streak of cloud,
The moon in the endless night no more alone.
In sunset hale of heart still:
In the autumn wind, risen from sickness.
There's always a place kept for an old horse
Though it can take no more to the long road.

Ch'ien and K'un are the symbols of the forces behind heaven and earth
in the divination system of the *Book of Changes*. The image is of a
solitary figure between sky and earth (with a suggestion of a scholar
poring over the *Book of Changes* ?).

Deep in Winter

Flower in the leaves, only as heaven pleases:
From Yangtse to brook, the same roots of stone.
Red cloud of morning's shadow likenesses:
The cold water on each touches its scar.
Easy, Yang Chu, to shed your tears:
Exile of Ch'u, hard to call back your ghost.
The waves in the wind are restless in the evening.
I put down my oar to lodge in what man's house?

Tu Fu is travelling by boat, evidently up some sidestream after leaving
the Yangtse. The 'flower in the leaves', as has long been recognized, is
the red sun against blue and violet clouds. 'Heaven' is both the power
which will bring back the flowers in spring (and perhaps good fortune
to Tu Fu) and the sky in which the illusory flower appears. There is a
sharp contrast between the images of lines 1, 3 and 2, 4, between the
insubstantial promise of spring in the sky and the wintery, stony, pre-
cisely visualized present with its scars of the past – the bases of stones
showing through water, the water rising to the marks stained at high
level.

The commentator Ch'ou Chao-ao (A.D. 1693) could make no sense
of the poem except by postulating a special verse form in which line 3
refers back to 1, 4 to 2, 7 to 5, 8 to 6. But it is likely, as Ch'ou Chao-ao
himself showed, that Tu Fu wrote the piece on his journey in 768–9
down the Yangtse, over Lake Tung-t'ing and up the Hsiang river. An
untranslated poem of 769, *Halt at K'ung-ling Bank*, refers to the red
rocks of Hsiang river as 'dawn-cloud stones'. The mysterious first
four lines can be read consecutively on the assumption that the roseate
clouds are conceived as emerging from the red rocks, in accordance
with the Chinese belief that clouds are breathed out by mountains and
stones. There is in fact a cliché 'roots of cloud' used of rocks, as in
Tu Fu's untranslated *Cliffs of Ch'ü-t'ang Gorges* (written in 766):

> Straight up into the sky, the rock face:
> Thrusting through the water, sudden roots of cloud.

Then 'roots of stone' in line 2, an idiom for the underwater base of stone, is revivified by the conjunction with 'flower', so that the cloud-flower grows out of the root of stone. The 'shadow likenesses' of line 3 are both the flower in the sky and the rocks which are likenesses of the clouds, and the 'each' of line 4 refers back to the latter sense.

Yang Chu (c. 350 B.C.) wept at the cross-roads because whichever road he chose would lead to a new cross-roads and multiply the chances of having lost his way. The 'exile of Ch'u' is the poet Ch'ü Yüan, drowned in Mi-lo river in the same region; the *Summons to the Soul*, one of the *Songs of Ch'u*, was traditionally understood as an appeal to his ghost to return to the world.

Autumn Meditation

Tu Fu wrote this sequence at K'uei-chou in 766: since he had arrived at Yün-an a little to the west in the previous year, this was his second autumn in the region ('The clustered chrysanthemums have opened twice'). K'uei-chou was a town adjoining and apparently no longer distinguished from Pai Ti (White Emperor City) on the Yangtse river, among mountains a little upstream from the Ch'ü-t'ang and Wu gorges. The eight poems, although not necessarily written at once, show a definite continuity. The first three give impressions of K'uei-chou over twenty-four hours, from morning to morning. In these Tu Fu is already thinking of Ch'ang-an far to the north; he imagines it beyond the Dipper in the night sky, and in bed thinks of night duty at the ministry *shang-shu sheng*, among maids burning incense and murals of ancient heroes. In the third poem the returning fisher-boats and the swallows not yet driven south by the cold remind him of his isolation and the political failures which led to it, and of his more successful friends, whom he imagines at Wu-ling (place of five Imperial mausolea) north of Ch'ang-an. The meditation now settles finally on Ch'ang-an, since 755 a 'chess-board' not only in appearance, with its grid of vertical and horizontal streets, but as the scene of a game won and lost in turn by loyalists, rebels, and Tibetan invaders. The last four poems recall scenes from the time of Ch'ang-an's greatness and of Tu Fu's own brief glory in the office of 'Reminder' at court (757–8).

I

Gems of dew wilt and wound the maple trees in the
   wood:
From Wu mountains, from Wu gorges, the air blows
   desolate.
The waves between the river banks merge in the seething
   sky,
Clouds in the wind above the passes touch their
   shadows on the ground.
Clustered chrysanthemums have opened twice, in tears
   of other days:
The forlorn boat, once and for all, tethers my homeward
   thoughts.
In the houses quilted clothes speed scissors and ruler.
The washing blocks pound, faster each evening, in Pai
   Ti high on the hill.

2

On the solitary walls of K'uei-chou the sunset rays slant,
Each night guided by the Dipper I gaze towards the
   capital.
It is true then that tears start when we hear the gibbon
   cry thrice:
Useless my mission adrift on the raft which came by
   this eighth month.
Fumes of the censers by the pictures in the ministry
   elude my sickbed pillow,
The whitewashed parapets of turrets against the hills
   dull the mournful bugles.
      Look! On the wall, the moon in the ivy
Already, by the shores of the isle, lights the blossoms on
   the reeds.

3

A thousand houses rimmed by the mountains are quiet
   in the morning light,
Day after day in the house by the river I sit in the blue
   of the hills.
Two nights gone the fisher-boats once more come
   bobbing on the waves,
Belated swallows in cooling autumn still flit to and fro.
. . . A disdained K'uang Heng, as a critic of policy:
As promoter of learning, a Liu Hsiang who failed.
Of the school-friends of my childhood, most did well.
By the Five Tombs in light cloaks they ride their sleek
   horses.

4

Well said Ch'ang-an looks like a chess-board:
A hundred years of the saddest news.
The mansions of princes and nobles all have new lords:
Another breed is capped and robed for office.
Due north on the mountain passes the gongs and drums
   shake,
To the chariots and horses campaigning in the west the
   winged dispatches hasten.
While the fish and the dragons fall asleep and the
   autumn river turns cold
My native country, untroubled times, are always in my
   thoughts.

5

The gate of P'eng-lai Palace faces the South Mountain:
Dew collects on the bronze stems out of the Misty River.
See in the west on Jasper Lake the Queen Mother
   descend:

Approaching from the east the purple haze fills the
  Han-ku pass.
The clouds roll back, the pheasant-tail screens open
  before the throne:
Scales ringed by the sun on dragon robes! I have seen
  the majestic face.
I lay down once by the long river, wake left behind by
  the years,
Who so many times answered the roll of court by the
  blue chain-patterned door.

6

From the mouth of Ch'üt-t'ang gorges here, to the side
  of Crooked River there,
For ten thousand miles of mist in the wind the touch of
  pallid autumn.
Through the walled passage from Calyx Hall the royal
  splendour coursed,
To Hibiscus Park the griefs of the frontier came.
Pearl blinds and embellished pillars closed in the yellow
  cranes,
Embroidered cables and ivory masts startled the white
  seagulls.
       Look back and pity the singing, dancing land!
Ch'in from most ancient times was the seat of princes.

7

K'un-ming Pool was the Han time's monument,
The banners of the Emperor Wu are here before my
  eyes.
Vega threads her loom in vain by night under the moon,
And the great stone fish's plated scales veer in the
  autumn wind.

The waves toss a zizania seed, over sunken clouds as
　　black:
Dew on the calyx chills the lotus, red with dropped
　　pollen.
　　　Over the pass, all the way to the sky, a road for
　　　　none but the birds.
On river and lakes, to the ends of the earth, one old
　　fisherman.

8

The K'un-wu road by Yü-su river ran its meandering
　　course,
The shadow of Purple Turret Peak fell into Lake
　　Mei-p'i.
Grains from the fragrant rice-stalks, pecked and dropped
　　by the parrots:
On the green *wu-t'ung* tree branches which the perching
　　phoenix aged.
Beautiful girls gathered kingfisher feathers for spring
　　gifts:
Together in the boat, a troop of immortals, we set forth
　　again in the evening. . . .
　　　This brush of many colours once forced the
　　　　elements.
Chanting, peering into the distance, in anguish my
　　white head droops.

Verse 2, lines 3, 4. The cries of gibbons in the gorges downstream
remind Tu Fu of a fisherman's song:

　　'Of the three gorges East of Pa the Wu gorge is longest,
　　When I hear the gibbon cry thrice the tears wet my clothes.'

　The moonlit river running straight to the sky suggests the legend
of a fisherman who saw a raft floating out to sea every year in the

eighth month (mid-autumn), mounted it, and was carried to the Milky Way, as well as the story of Chang Ch'ien, sent as ambassador to the West by the Emperor Wu of Han, who rode on a raft to the source of the Yellow River and similarly found himself in the Milky Way. Tu Fu implies that he is drifting farther from instead of nearer to the heavens (i.e. the court).

Verse 5, lines 1–4. Tu Fu refers to P'eng-lai Palace in Ch'ang-an, named after one of the islands of immortals in the Eastern sea; the pillars erected by Wu of Han to collect dew for the elixir (cf. Li Ho's *Bronze Immortal*. The Misty River is the empyrean); the Western Queen Mother (Hsi-wang-mu) who banqueted King Mu (1001–947 B.C.) at Jasper Lake in her country far to the west, an incident which the poet fuses with her later descent from the sky to teach the arts of immortality to Wu of Han; the philosopher Lao-tzŭ coming through the passes preceded by a purple cloud on his final journey to the west.

Verse 7, lines 1–4. K'un-ming Pool near Ch'ang-an was made by Wu of Han for naval exercises. Near it was a statue of the Weaver Girl (the star Vega) and in it a stone whale with movable fins and tail.

Meng Chiao (751–814)

Meng Chiao was the eldest and perhaps the best of the circle which centred on Han Yü. His bare, bleak style is well summed up in a couplet in which he contrasts it with his friend's:

> The bones of poetry jut in Meng Chiao,
> The waves of poetry surge in Han Yü.

Many have detested what Su Shih (Su Tung-p'o, 1036–1101) described as his 'cold cicada's call', although the filial sentiment of *Wanderer's Song* has made it a popular anthology piece. Cold is indeed almost his central image – the bracing chill of high mountains, the misery of cold weather in poverty and sickness.

Meng Chiao's poetry shows a new boldness in imagery characteristic of Han Yü's circle. Many of his expressions are extremely violent to Chinese ears – the wind 'combing' his bones, the spray on rocks compared with the spittle of the hungry ghosts of the drowned, the mountain which 'stuffs all heaven and earth', with the sun and moon 'growing up from its stones'.

Sadness of the Gorges
(Third of ten)

Above the gorges, one thread of sky:
Cascades in the gorges twine a thousand cords.
High up, the slant of splintered sunlight, moonlight:
Beneath, curbs to the wild heave of the waves.
The shock of a gleam, and then another,
In depths of shadow frozen for centuries:
The rays between the gorges do not halt at noon;
Where the straits are perilous, more hungry spittle.
Trees lock their roots in rotted coffins
And the twisted skeletons hang tilted upright:
Branches weep as the frost perches
Mournful cadences, remote and clear.
     A spurned exile's shrivelled guts
Scald and seethe in the water and fire he walks through.
A lifetime's like a fine-spun thread,
The road goes up by the rope at the edge.
When he pours his libation of tears to the ghosts in the
     stream
The ghosts gather, a shimmer on the waves.

An Excursion to the Dragon Pool Temple on Chung-nan

A place which the flying birds do not reach,
A monastery set on the summit of Chung-nan.
The water where the dragon dwells is always blue:
The mountain since the rain lifted is fresher still.
I came out on foot above the white sun,
Sit leaning over the brink of the clear brook.
The soil is cold, the pines and cassias stunted:
The rocks are steep, the path turns off course.
When the evening chimes send off the departing guest
The notes I count drop from the farthest sky.

Stopping on a Journey at the East Water Pavilion at Lo-ch'eng

Colours of water and bamboo wash each other,
Blue blossoms stir on the pillars of the porch.
The wind which roams without design
Cleanses of passion's transient strife.
In the fall of the frost the leaves have a parched sound,
Chilled by the scene men's talk cools.
Since I came to this abbey Hermit's Summons
For a while the dust weighs lightly on my cloak.

On Mount Ching

Gadflies swarm on the weary horse.
Streaming blood, it can go no further.
The colour of night rises on the road behind:
Ahead, uphill, hear the tiger roar.
These times, the traveller's heart
Is a flag a hundred feet high in the wind.

Wanderer's Song

The thread in the hand of a kind mother
Is the coat on the wanderer's back.
Before he left she stitched it close
In secret fear that he would be slow to return.
Who will say that the inch of grass in his heart
Is gratitude enough for all the sunshine of spring?

Song of the Old Man of the Hills

I never go to the plains beneath the hills,
Only on the hillside plant my fields.
The hatchet at my waist chops down the pines in the
copse,
The gourd in my hand draws water from the homestead
spring.
What do I care for the force of written words?
Let no one heed the shifts of sun and moon.
When the twisted tree at last shall be my body
Then I shall begin to live out my natural span.

Wandering on Mount Chung-nan

South Mountain stuffs all heaven and earth,
Sun and moon grow up from its stones.
The high peak at night holds back the sun,
The deep vales are never bright by day.
Natural for mountain people to grow straight:
Where paths are steep the mind levels.
A long wind drives the pines and cypresses
With a sound which sweeps the thousand hollows clean.
Who comes here regrets that he ever studied
Morning after morning, to be close to floating fame.

Line 3. Note (by Meng Chiao himself?): 'To the West of T'ai-po
peak one sees the sun lingering after twilight.'

Complaint of a Neglected Wife

My reproach is like the mottled bamboo:
Anguished roots twist beneath.
Before the shoot was out of the ground
Already it bore the scars of secret tears.

The speckles on bamboos are the stains of the tears of the two goddesses of the Hsiang river mourning the death of their husband the Emperor Shun.

Impromptu

Keep away from sharp swords,
Don't go near a lovely woman.
A sharp sword too close will wound your hand,
Woman's beauty too close will wound your life.
The danger of the road is not in the distance,
Ten yards is far enough to break a wheel.
The peril of love is not in loving too often,
A single evening can leave its wound in the soul.

Autumn Thoughts
(Two of fifteen)

2

The face of the autumn moon freezes.
Old and homeless, will and force are spent.
The drip of the chill dew breaks off my dream,
The cold wind harshly combs my bones.
On the mat, the print of a sickly contour:
Writhing cares twist in my belly.
Doubtful thoughts find nothing to lean on:
I listen at the least stir, and am disappointed.
The *wu-t'ung* wilted, looming high,
Sounds and echoes like strings sadly plucked.

5

Wind and bamboos strum and speak to each other,
Noises in the gloom of this secluded chamber.
Phantoms crowd my dimmed hearing,
Blurred sight strains to make things out.
Dry rain of leaves drops on the note *shang*,
Quilted for autumn I lie under flimsy cloud:
My sick bones have hacking edges,
The poem shapes out of a dreary mumble.
Meagre and wrinkled, wilted as these,
Sinking manhood has followed the westward sun.
Useless to call the spiralling wisp of a life
One strand in the web that heaven and earth weave.

Verse 5, lines 5, 6. '*Shang*': the note corresponding to autumn in the pentatonic scale. 'Flimsy cloud'; the autumn of north China has thin cloud high in a clear cold sky.

The Stones where the Haft Rotted

Wang Chih of the Chin dynasty (265–419) went into the moun-
tains (Stone Bridge Mountain) to gather firewood, and saw two
boys playing chess. The boys gave him a thing like a date stone,
which he ate, and satisfied his hunger. At the end of the game, the
boys pointed and said: 'Look! Your axe-handle is rotten.' When
Chih returned to his village, he was a hundred years old.

Less than a day in paradise,
And a thousand years have passed among men.
While the pieces are still being laid on the board
All things have changed to emptiness.
The woodman takes the road home,
The haft of his axe has rotted in the wind:
Nothing is what it was but the stone bridge
Still spanning a rainbow cinnabar-red.

Han Yü (768–824)

Han Yü was the leader of the 'Old Prose' movement, which reacted against the formal and elaborate 'Parallel Prose' dominant for some centuries. The complexity and rigid parallelism of New Style verse had exposed the fact, for long obscured, that verse and prose have different resources; Han Yü rediscovered the possibilities of the simple, strong, and flexible style of ancient prose, and used it as his weapon in defence of Confucianism against Buddhism. The Confucian revival which he initiated was the first step towards the permanent victory over Buddhism completed by the Neo-Confucian philosophers of the Sung dynasty (960–1279).

Han Yü was an essayist and polemicist rather than a poet; but his verse, although sometimes prosy, was both original and influential. Conscious that T'ang poetry had already passed its high point, he did not hope to equal Li Po and Tu Fu, but strove to be different. After the New Style imposed its laws of parallelism and tone sequence on the traditional eight-line verse, the Old Style had started on a different course. Li Po and Tu Fu already wrote Old Style poems of greater length and varying numbers of syllables to the line; Han Yü and his follower Lu T'ung, almost alone among T'ang poets, based their reputations primarily on long poems, for which they adopted devices formerly confined to prose and the *fu* (prose poem), the free use of explicit similes, lines without caesura, sentences running past the couplet, unpoetical subject matter. Sixty lines of Han Yü's *South Mountain* display forty-six similes introduced by 'like' (all reproduced here by a 'like', 'as', or 'as though'). The nineteenth-century scholar Liu Hsi-tsai remarked on Han Yü's power to 'make beauty out of ugliness'; examples noticed by a recent critic, Su Hsüeh-lin, include descriptions of an execution, of the demons of pestilence feeding on the dung and vomit of the sick, of a friend snoring. (The most striking example in the poems translated here is Lu T'ung's picture of the giant frog swallowing the nine suns.)

The feature which has always distinguished Han Yü's circle for Chinese readers is a taste for 'strange' and 'daring' imagery, for conceits, fantasy, and grotesquery. We have already noticed this tendency in Meng Chiao, who in other respects is closer to the main T'ang tradition. Such images seldom strike a Westerner as especially daring, and except in Meng Chiao they are often tinsel, without the resonance of the imagery of Tu Fu, Li Ho, and Li Shang-yin. One may well agree with most Chinese opinion that this episode was an aberration, since it sacrificed the concentration which is the real strength of Chinese poetry for a more open texture which is better suited to our own. Although I have translated nothing which I do not enjoy, either as poetry or simply as fun, the school would earn less space if it were not for the interest of watching the Chinese tradition momentarily straying in the direction of our own.

Conceited poetry was not the only kind written at the turn of the century, even in Han Yü's circle. Po Chü-i (772–846) was the most important representative of another tendency of the period. With his friend Yüan Chen (779–831) he recalled attention to the social and human content of poetry and cultivated a deliberately plain style, equally averse to fanciful imagery and to the formal restrictions of the New Style. But we need not consider Po Chü-i further, since he is already, through Waley's translations, the Chinese poet best known and best loved in the West.

Autumn Thoughts
(Ninth of eleven)

A frosty wind harries the *wu-t'ung*,
The crowded leaves stick wilting to the tree.
On the empty step one piece drops
With a crackle like a crushed gem.
'His night breath is spent', I say,
'Wang Shu has made his globe a meteor
In the blue void, resting on nothing,
Flying a course dangerous and hard to hold.'
I wake with a start, go to the door, look out,
Lean on the pillar, long my tears flow:
Grief and care have wasted the shadow on the dial,
Sun and moon are like a juggler's balls.
Back to the missed road, however far:
It is for you he stopped his dusty saddle.

'Night breath': the energies accumulated during the night, with
which we wake fresh in the morning. Wang Shu, the charioteer of the
moon, naturally has to dissipate his.

A Withered Tree

Not a twig or a leaf on the old tree,
Wind and frost harm it no more.
A man could pass through the hole in its belly,
Ants crawl searching under its peeling bark.
Its only lodger, the toadstool which dies in a morning,
The birds no longer visit in the twilight.
But its wood can still spark tinder.
It does not care yet to be only the void at its heart.

The 'void at its heart' is both the hollow inside of the tree and the
Buddhist ideal of the mind freed from the illusion of a material body.

Evening: for Chang Chi and Chou K'uang

The sunlight thins, the view empties:
Back from a walk, I lie under the front eaves.
Fairweather clouds like torn fluff
And the new moon like a whetted sickle.
A zest for the fields and moors stirs in me,
The ambition for robes of office has long since turned
    to loathing.
While I live, shall I take your hand again
Sighing that our years will soon be done?

From The South Mountains

(Three extracts from a poem of 102 couplets, all ending on the same rhyme, about the mountains south of the capital Ch'ang-an, including Chung-nan (South Mountain) and T'ai-po.)

(i)
Gazing as I climbed a high peak
I saw them huddle closer together,
Angles and corners jutting as the air brightened,
Emerging patterns in a needlework;
Or interfused in a steamy haze
Pierced through by sudden glimpses of heights and
    depths
As it drifted at random, winnowed without a wind,
And dissipated to warm the tender growths.
Sometimes a level plain of cloud settled
With scattered peaks exposed above,
Long eyebrows floating in the empty sky,
The lustrous green of paint newly touched up;
And a single strut of broken crag protruded,
The upreared beak of the Roc as it bathes in the sea.

In spring when the Yang waters in secret
And from deep within breathes up the glistening shoots,
Though cliff and crag loom tall against the sky
Their outlines soften like a drunken face.
In summer's flames, when the trees are at their prime
Dense and shady, and deeper bury the hills,
The magic spirit day by day exhales
A breath which issues in the shaping clouds.

While the autumn frosts delight in punishing
The hills stand starved and stripped, with wasted flanks
And sharp edges which zigzag across the horizon,
In inflexible pride scorning the universe.
Though winter's element is inky black
The ice and snow are master jewellers,
And the light of dawn shines over the dangerous peaks
Constant wide and high for a thousand miles.
In daylight or darkness never a fixed posture,
From moment to moment always a different scene.

(ii)
North of the great lake of K'un-ming,
On a brilliant day, I came to view the mountain.
It dropped straight down as far as I could see
Trapped wrongside up and steeped in the clear water.
When ripples stirred on the face of the pool
The rowdy monkeys hopped and skipped,
Shrieked with amazement to see their shattered shapes,
Looked up and gaped with relief that they had not fallen
    in.

(iii)
Fine weather since yesterday.
My old ambition is satisfied at last.
I've clambered all the way to the topmost peak,
Scurrying with the flying-squirrels and the weasels.
The road dips in front, the vista opens
Far and wide over crowded bumps and wrinkles,
Lined up in files like processions
Or crouched like grappling fighters,
Or laid low, as though prostrate in submission,
Or starting up like crowing pheasants;

Scattered like loose tiles
Or running together like converging spokes,
Off keel like rocking boats
Or in full stride like horses at the gallop;
Back to back as though offended,
Face to face as though lending a hand,
Tangled like sprouting bamboos
Or piled like moxa on a wound;
Neatly composed like a picture,
Curly like ancient script,
Constellated like stars,
Conglomerated like stationary clouds,
Surging like billows,
Crumbling like hoed soil,
   And some like champions, Fen or Yü,
When the stakes are down, eager for the prize ahead,
The foremost and strongest rearing high above,
The losers looking foolish and speechless with rage;
Or like some majestic Emperor
And the vassals gathered in his court,
Even the nearest not too familiar,
Even the furthest never insubordinate;
Or like guests seated at a table
With the banquet spread before them,
Or like a cortège on the way to the graveyard
Carrying the coffin to the tomb:
     And some in rows like pots
With others sticking up behind like vases:
Some carapaced like basking turtles,
Slumped like sleeping animals,
Wriggling like dragons fleeing into hiding,
Spreading wings like pouncing vultures;

Side by side like friends and equals,
Ranked as though in due degree,
Shooting apart like falling spray
Or introducing themselves like lodgers in an inn;
Aloof as enemies
Or intimate as man and wife,
Dignified as tall hats
Or flippant as waving sleeves,
Commanding like fortresses
Or hemmed in like hunted prey;
Draining away to the East
Or reclining with heads to the North,
Like flames in the kitchen stove,
Like the steam of a cooking dinner;
Marchers who will not halt
And the stragglers left behind,
Leaning posts which do not topple,
Unstrung bows which no one draws,
Bare like bald pates,
Smoking like pyres;
Unevenly cracked like diviners' tortoiseshells
Or split into layers like hexagrams,
Level across the front like Po ☰☰
Or broken at the back like Kou. ☰☰☰

Lu T'ung (died 835)

Lu T'ung, who called himself Yü-ch'uan-tzŭ (Philosopher of Jade River), took the poetry of fancy farther than any other T'ang poet. Although he has never been regarded as more than a minor writer, his *Eclipse* has kept a modest place in Chinese literature as a unique and freakish curiosity. Han Yü himself made an abridged and rather tamer version of it.

The *Eclipse* is a political allegory, in which 'Heaven' is the Emperor, and the moon, the night-time 'eye of Heaven', is an eclipsed minister who has never been convincingly identified. The date is 810. Lu T'ung considers, in turn, various explanations of the catastrophe – that the sun (the chief minister?) has eaten the moon, that Heaven has blinded itself by gazing too long at earthly beauty (the Emperor has been misled by a favourite concubine?) – and finally decides in favour of the explanation of popular folklore, that the moon has been swallowed by a giant frog (the eunuchs?). The translation breaks off nearly half way through the poem, without omissions up to this point. Lu T'ung continues with a memorial to Heaven advising the punishment of a long series of negligent functionaries beginning with the dragon of the East, bird of the South, tiger of the West, and tortoise of the North, and concludes with the happy passing of the eclipse.

Politics was literally the death of Lu T'ung; he was executed in 835 for supposed complicity in the Kan-lu rebellion.

The Eclipse of the Moon

> The fifth year of the new Son of Heaven,
> The cyclic year Keng-yin;
> The season when the handle of the Dipper
> sticks into Aries,
> The month when the pitch-tube is Yellow
> Bell.

Ten thousand forest trees stood rigid in the night:
The cold air tensed against us, solid and windless.
The glittering silver dish rose from the bottom of the
sea,
Came forth and lighted the East of my thatched cottage.
On heaven's smooth and violet surface the freezing
light stopped flowing,
Rays from the ice pierced and crossed the cold glimmer
of moonrise.

> At first it seemed that a white lotus
> Had floated up from the Dragon King's palace.
> But this night, the fifteenth of the eighth month,
> Was not like other nights;
> For now we saw a strange thing:
> There was something eating its way inside the rim.

The rim was as though a strong man hacked off pieces
with an axe,
The cassia was like a snowy peak dragged and tumbled
by the wind.
The mirror refined a hundredfold
Till it shone right through to the gall
Suddenly was buried in cold ash:
The pearl of the fiery dragon

Which flew up out of its brain
Went back into the oyster's womb.
Ring and disc crumbled away as I watched,
Darkness smeared the whole sky like soot,
Rubbing out in an instant the last tracks,
And then it seemed that for thousands of ages the sky
    would never open.
        Who would guess that a thing so magical
        Could be so discomfited?
        The stars came out like sprinkled sand
        Disputing which could shine the brightest,
        And the lamps lit by the servants
        With a dusky glow like tortoiseshell
        This night spat flames like long rainbows
        Shooting from the houses through holes and cracks
            into a thousand roads.

Yü-ch'uan-tzŭ's tears fell in the middle courtyard
As he walked alone,
And reflected that the sun and moon
Are the essence of Primal Yang and Primal Yin.
Because High Heaven must know how the world goes
It brought forth the sun and moon
For the unremitting toil of running across the sky
Serving as heaven's eyes and sending down the light.
If these eyes go unprotected
When the Lord of Heaven walks the Way by what shall
    he set his course?

I know how the school of Yin and Yang explains it:
'When the mid-month sun devours the moon the
    moonlight is quenched,

When the new moon covers the sun the sunlight fails.'
But the two eyes do not attack each other;
This theory does not convince me.
Better what Lao-tzŭ said, who taught Confucius:
'The five colours blind men's eyes.'
I fear that Heaven, just like man,
Can lose its sight by lusting after beauty.
But the time is wrong, it is not spring,
All things have passed their prime of loveliness,
The blue of the hills is the colour of broken shards,
The ice piles mountain-high on the green water,
The flowers have withered, their woman's charm all
    gone,
The birds are dead, their songs vanished.
In brutish winter what is there to love
For Heaven to gaze on till an eye goes blind?

There is another ancient tale I know
Of a demon frog which comes to eat the moon.
If the disc a thousand miles wide has gone down into
    your belly
Who was the dam that bore you, ignorant brute?
Can it be that, risen from the caves of the sea,
You have learned to climb the blue void?
I fear it was you that, in an eyelid's blink,
Blotted out what took so long to grow.
The Yellow Emperor had two pairs of eyes,
Emperor Shun saw clear through double pupils;
When either Emperor focused his four eyes
The beams spread all the way to the four seas.
I was born too late to meet these Emperors,
Their history is doubtful, we cannot be certain,

85

But would they have ever suffered in patience
While insects and reptiles played tricks with their
    pupils?
A long sigh for the white hare which pounds the magic
    herb
To no other end than to guard from crimes and treasons;
The medicine is made and the mortar full but the blend
    has turned out wrong,
See what happens when you trust the white hare!

Think how once, when Yao was Heaven,
Ten suns burned the Nine Regions.
Metals fused into streaming quicksilver,
Jade cooked to charred cinnabar,
The baking universe became a kiln.
A hundred cares oppressed Yao's heart,
God saw the cares of Yao's heart,
And in sudden fury let loose a mighty torrent,
Planning to drown in the flood the monsters of the nine
    new suns.
High up into heaven the suns ran, out of reach of the
    flood;
There was nothing to see in a myriad kingdoms but
    teeming babies growing fishes' heads.
At this time nine charioteers drove the nine suns,
Each with an ensign in his hand and flourishing token
    streamers.
Harnessed to the chariots were six times nine, fifty-four
    young and scaly and hornless dragons,
Lightning-swift, at the nine fiery shafts.
If then you had bitten jagged edges across the wheels,
Grabbed reins and ropes, and scratched and clawed,

Crammed them rumbling down into your gullet,
Crimson scales and fiery birds stinging your mouth
    with burns,
Wings and back-fins upended and sideways sucked down
    with a gurgling noise,
Propping your belly up as it bulged with lumps like
    mountains and hillocks,
Then you could have gorged yourself to death and
    been done with thieving,
Not only stuffed your hungry pit
But also freed Yao's heart of cares.
It rankles that when you should have eaten
You buried your head and had no appetite;
But now that you should not eat
With lips stretched wide and gaping jaws you eat
    insatiably.
You have fed your disobedience by eating the eye of
    Heaven.
How long before the God on High ordains your
    execution?

Alas, that the tiger's breeder
By the tiger is mauled,
That Heaven, which pampered the frog,
By the frog is blinded!
Know then that favour to those not our kind
Time and again brings ruin on ourselves.

Every man I know whose eyes ailed him
Went looking for a sound doctor to treat them;
Heaven, I suppose, is no different from man,
And will surely miss an eye as much as we do.

Is it possible that the Lady in the Moon
Will study the art of Doctor P'ien Ch'iao,
Seize hold of a lancet rammed down that throat,
And rid Heaven of the sty above its pupil?

At first there was still a glimmer.
For a long time now it has been like a coat of lacquer.
I only fear that his work is done
And never again will he vomit it up.

Li Ho (791–817)

Li Ho is the most remarkable case in Chinese literature of a poet recently rediscovered after long neglect. He does not appear at all in the most familiar anthologies, such as the eighteenth-century *Three Hundred T'ang Poems*. Although famous in the ninth century and never quite forgotten, he offended the conventionality of later taste by his individuality and its health and balance by his morbidity and violence. To see his peculiar qualities as virtues required the breakdown of traditional literary standards in the nineteenth and twentieth centuries. It is now widely recognized by Chinese, Japanese, and Western readers alike that he is a major poet both in his own right and as a creative influence, the link between Han Yü, who discovered his talent when he was still a boy, and the masters of the ninth century, Tu Mu, who wrote the preface to his poems, and Li Shang-yin, who wrote his biography.

Li Ho continued the cult of 'strange' imagery, but turned it into something which is strange by any standards, not merely by those of the world's most sensible and temperate poetic tradition. He also continued Han Yü's experiments in Old Style versification, showing a taste for unorthodox rhyme schemes and for sequences of three or four quatrains rather than the standard eight-line form, the transitions between lines often so abrupt that he was credited with compiling his poems out of independently written couplets. These features he combines with an extreme compression more characteristic of the New Style verse of Tu Fu.

Li Ho's central theme is the transience of life, a subject which he treats as though no one before him had ever felt the drip of the water-clock on his nerves, in a wholly personal imagery of ghosts, blood, dying animals, weeping statues, whirlwinds, the will-o'-the-wisp – the last appears in many guises, 'ghostly lamps', 'cold blue candle-flames', 'sinister fires', 'darkened torches', 'fireflies in the tomb'. He seems quite uninterested in any of the common recipes for reconciliation with death, Confucian, Taoist, or Buddhist, with the result that he is equally far from the serenity of the greatest Chinese poets and the facile melancholy of the more commonplace. Even in his recurrent visions of the Taoist paradise he imagines the immortals dying, and his fantasies of watching from heaven the land and sea changing places over thousands of years only sharpen his sense of the irrevocable passage of time on earth. In the untranslated *Second Year of Chang-ho* he wishes long life to the Emperor, yet finishes with the disturbing and characteristic qualification:

> . . . Till the thread of the Seven Stars snaps and the Lady in the Moon dies.

An aphorism often repeated in various forms declares that Tu Fu's genius was that of a Confucian sage and Li Po's of a Taoist immortal, that Po Chü-i's was human and Li Ho's ghostly or daemonic. An obsession with the world of spirits and of the dead shows up in many of his poems and accounts for his interest in shamanistic seances and in the *Songs of Ch'u* of the third century B.C., almost the only earlier poetry which shows a similar concern.[1] One has the impression that Li Ho, who died young, felt himself already half way across the boundary between the living and the dead. But being Chinese, he has no place in his imagination for our own favourite bogey, the abstraction 'Death'.

A more radical novelty of Li Ho, in which he looks for-

1. The Songs of Ch'u are translated in full in David Hawkes, *Ch'u T'ẑü: Songs of the South* (1959). Cf. also Waley's *Nine Songs* (1955) and the 'Hymn to the Fallen' and 'Great Summons' in his *Chinese Poems*.

ward to Li Shang-yin, is an unobtrusive change in the relation between subjective and objective. A rigour in seeking the objective correlative of emotion is a strong point of most Chinese poetry in all periods. However, such a poet as Tu Fu constantly reminds us of his existence, recalling his past, bewailing his present, seeing images of his loneliness in a solitary cloud or a fisherman in an empty landscape. He will even on occasion speak of his feelings, or at any rate his tears, with a simplicity which falls rather flat in English. One of his most famous later poems, *Climbing Yüeh-yang Tower*, is not in this volume because I can find no better equivalent for the last line than

As I lean on the balcony my tears stream down.

Li Ho's more characteristic poems seldom introduce him directly at all, only sights, sounds, and smells. The tears in his poems are shed by flowers, by a rainy sky, by exorcized goblins who weep blood. But in spite of this reticence one is never in doubt of the pressure of an emotion which not only selects but exaggerates, distorts, invents the impressions which the poet offers to our senses, and of a muffled violence which erupts in the paranoid fury of *Don't Go Out of the Door*. Because of this unvarying stamp of a unique personality Li Ho is detached at a much shallower level than is Tu Fu. Tu Fu, in spite of his personal references, does not at bottom ask us to be interested in anything particular to himself; he selects the universal in his experience and invites us to sympathize, not with him, but with a generalized figure of man in exile.

Li Ho reminds many readers of Baudelaire. The affinity is not altogether an illusion, but in one respect it can mislead. When we read that Li Ho was called a *kuei ts'ai*, a ghostly or daemonic genius, and notice his apparently familiar constellation of pessimism, voluptuousness, aestheticism, and an imagination haunted by dark forces, it is tempting to read him as a nineteenth-century Satanist. But the Western sense of evil of course assumes a Christian background, and the *kuei* of Li Ho's poems are generally not devils but ghosts, sad rather than malevolent beings. Nor are there any overtones of the flesh and the devil in Li Ho's sensuality, which may be disreputable for a strict Confucian, but hardly sinful. His pessimism also has none of the ambivalence which one expects in a Western artist obsessed by original sin, who is at least half on the side of the destructive element because he finds it at the bottom of his own heart.

The Liang Terrace

Terrace and pool of the Prince of Liang stand up in
mid-sky:
Every night the Milky Way flies down into the water.
In front of the terrace mortised jades shape interlocking
dragons,
And the powdered green bamboos sweep heaven
grieving in the dew.

He drank wine to the chime of bells and shot his arrows
at heaven,
In his furs braided with gold tigers and streaked with
spurted blood.
Morning after morning, evening after evening, he
sighed when the seas turned round,
And he tethered the sun on a long rope that youth might
never pass.

The clotted red of hibiscus blossoms changed to the tint
of autumn,
Faces of orchids as spring departed cried noiseless tears:
Migrant geese in the reeds of the isles proclaimed that
spring had come,
In the slime of desolate moors the floods of autumn
whitened.

Magic Strings

The witch pours the libation, clouds fill the sky,
In the flaming coals of the jade brazier the fumes of
    incense throb.
The God of the Sea and the Hill Nymph take their
    places,
Votive papers rustle in the howling whirlwind.
On her inlaid lute of passion-wood a goldleaf phoenix
    dances:
With knitted brow at each muttered phrase she plucks
    the strings once.
She calls to the stars and summons the demons to taste
    of her dish and cup:
Mankind shudders when the mountain goblins feed.
The glow of the sun behind Chung-nan hangs low in a
    trough of the hills:
The gods are here, for ever present between somewhere
    and nowhere!
The gods scold, the gods are pleased, in spasms on the
    medium's face.
— Then the gods with a myriad outriders go back to the
    blue mountains.

A Piece for Magic Strings

(A shamaness exorcizes baleful creatures.)

On the western hills the sun sets, the eastern hills darken,
Horses blown by the whirlwind tread the clouds.
From coloured lute and plain pipes, crowded faint notes:
Her flowered skirt rustles as she steps in the autumn
   dust.
When the wind brushes the cassia leaves and a cassia
   seed drops
The blue racoon weeps blood and the cold fox dies.
Dragons painted on the ancient wall with tails of inlaid
   gold
The God of Rain rides into the autumn pool;
And the owl a hundred years old, which changed to a
   goblin of the trees,
Hears the sound of laughter as green flames start up
   inside its nest.

On and on for ever

The white glare recedes to the Western hills,
High in the distance sapphire blossoms rise.
Where shall there be an end of old and new?
A thousand years have whirled away in the wind.
The sands of the ocean change to stone,
Fishes puff bubbles at the bridge of Ch'in.
The empty shine streams on into the distance,
The bronze pillars melt away with the years.

'Sapphire blossoms': blue moonlit clouds?
   'Bridge of Ch'in': Shih-huang-ti, who founded the Ch'in dynasty in 221 B.C., is said to have tried to build a bridge over the sea in order to see where the sun rises; spirits pulled it down as he was building it.
   'Bronze pillars'; those which supported the bronze immortals which collected dew for the elixir (cf. *A Bronze Immortal takes Leave of Han*), and/or the bronze pillar on Mount K'un-lun which holds up the sky.

On the Frontier

A Tartar horn tugs at the north wind,
Thistle Gate shines whiter than the stream.
The sky swallows the road to Kokonor.
On the Great Wall, a thousand miles of moonlight.

The dew comes down, the banners drizzle,
Cold bronze rings the watches of the night.
The nomads' armour meshes serpents' scales.
Horses neigh, Evergreen Mound's champed white.

In the still of autumn see the Pleiades.
Far out on the sands, danger in the furze.
North of their tents is surely the sky's end
Where the sound of the river streams beyond the border.

'Evergreen Mound': tomb of Wang Chao-chün, concubine of
the Emperor Yüan of Han (48–33 B.C.), who gave her as wife to a
Tartar Khan; the grass always grew on her tomb.
    'Pleiades': their flickering was an omen of nomad invasion.

The Northern Cold

The sky glows one side black, three sides purple.
The Yellow River's ice closes, fish and dragons die.
Bark three inches thick cracks across the grain,
Carts a hundred piculs heavy mount the river's water.
Flowers of frost on the grass are as big as coins,
Brandished swords will not pierce the foggy sky,
Crashing ice flies in the swirling seas,
And cascades hang noiseless in the mountains, rainbows
    of jade.

An Arrowhead from the ancient Battlefield of Ch'ang-p'ing

Lacquer dust and powdered bone and red cinnabar grains:
From the spurt of ancient blood the bronze has flowered.
White feathers and gilt shaft have melted away in the rain,
Leaving only this triple-cornered broken wolf's tooth.

I was searching the plain, riding with two horses,
In the stony fields east of the post-station, on a bank where bamboos sprouted,
After long winds and brief daylight, beneath the dreary stars,
Damped by a black flag of cloud which hung in the empty night.

To left and right, in the air, in the earth, ghosts shrieked from wasted flesh.
The curds drained from my upturned jar, mutton victuals were my sacrifice.
Insects settled, the wild geese swooned, the buds were blight-reddened on the reeds,
The whirlwind was my escort, puffing sinister fires.

In tears, seeker of ancient things, I picked up this broken barb
With snapped point and russet flaws, which once pierced through flesh.
In the east quarter on South Street a pedlar on horseback
Talked me into bartering the metal for a votive basket.

99

Sing Loud

The south wind's gust against the hill will make it flat
    land,
By God's appointment T'ien Wu shifts the waters of
    the sea.
When the Queen Mother's peach blossoms turn red
    the thousandth time
Grandfather P'eng and Wizard Hsien will have died
    how many deaths?

By the dark hairs of the piebald horse the dapple's edge
    meanders,
Graceful spring's willows are closed in yellow mist.
The lute-girl coaxes me with the gold-handled cup.
Before my blood and spirit fused, who was I?

No sense in wildly drinking, Governor Ting!
The time's best men don't stick to one master.
When I buy silk I shall have them embroider the Lord
    of P'ing-yüan,
When I have wine I shall pour libations only on the soil
    of Chao.

The clock drips fast and the water chokes the jade frog:
The girl of Wei's tresses thin, she will not risk the comb.
See how autumn eyebrows have changed to new green.
Why all that thrusting and shoving when we were
    twenty?

Stanza 1. The wind slowly wears away the hills; T'ien Wu, god of the
waters, is gradually exchanging the sea and the dry land. The peaches
of the Western Queen Mother (Hsi-wang-mu), the food of the

immortals, flower once in three thousand years – how many lifetimes of P'eng Tsu (the Chinese Methuselah) or of the shaman Hsien who knew the hour of every man's death?

Stanza 3. I am out of office, but perhaps I shall find another patron like the Lord of P'ing-yüan in Chao in the third century B.C. who supported several thousand clients. (The name 'Governor Ting' appears as a nonsense syllable in folksong.)

Stanza 4. The third line is highly ambiguous. Chinese idiom uses 'eyebrow' for crescent-shaped leaves (willow, cassia. cf. Li Shang-yin's *Willow*); it also allows the conceit of calling fresh, youthful hair green; and a green eyebrow paint was used by women (cf. Li Ho's *Dawn in Stone City*, Han Yü's *South Mountains*, lines 11, 12).

Bring in the Wine

A glass goblet
Deep-tinted amber.
Crimson pearls drip from the wine-cask,
Boiling dragon and roasting phoenix weep jades of fat.
Silken screens and embroidered curtains close in the
    scented breeze.
    Blow the dragon flute,
    Beat the lizard-skin drum.
    White teeth sing,
    Slender waists dance.
More than ever now, as the green spring nears its
    evening,
And peach flowers scatter like crimson rain!
Be advised by me, stay drunken all your life:
Wine does not reach the earth on Liu Ling's grave.

Liu Ling: most famous of Chinese drunkards.

Autumn Comes

For base and noble the same end
When every ambition's won or lost.
Galloping waves urge on the endless night,
Falling dew hurries the brief dawn.

From *Song of the Underworld* (Tai k'ao-li hsing) by Pao Chao
(414–66).

The wind in the *wu-t'ung* startles the heart, a lusty man
    despairs;
Spinners in the fading lamplight cry chill silk.
Who will study a bamboo book still green
And forbid the grubs to bore their powdery holes?
This night's thoughts will surely stretch my guts
    straight:
Cold in the rain a sweet phantom comes to console the
    writer.
By the autumn tombs a ghost chants the poem of Pao
    Chao.
My angry blood for a thousand years will be emeralds
    under the earth!

'Spinners': a common name for crickets, because their hum
(incidentally, like the wind shedding the leaves of the *wu-t'ung*, a
typically autumn sound) resembles that of the spinning wheel. 'Cry
chill silk' is as violent an expression in Chinese as in this literal render-
ing (cf. the tamer 'weep the sky's sheen' in *A Dream of Heaven*).

:Bamboo book': a classic, an immortal book. Books were written
on bamboo until the discovery of paper. Cf. Tu Fu, *Autumn Wastes*
No. 3, Li Ho, *Musing*.

'Emeralds'. Ch'ang Hung (*c.* 500 B.C.) was unjustly executed;
his blood changed to emerald within three years as a sign of his
innocence.

A Dream of Heaven

The old hare and the chilled frog weep the sky's sheen,
Through a door ajar in a mansion of cloud the rays slant
    white on the wall.
The white-jade wheel shivers the dew into wet globes
    of light;
Chariot bells meet girdle pendants on cassia-scented
    paths.

Yellow dust and clear water beneath the Fairy Mountains
Change places once in a thousand years which pass like
    galloping horses.
When you peer at far-off China, nine puffs of smoke:
And the single pool of the ocean has drained into a cup.

The frog, the hare which pounds the elixir of life and the cassia tree
are all on the moon.

'Chariot bells': men out driving meet girls walking with jade
pendants tinkling at their waists.

The 'nine puffs of smoke' are generally identified with the nine
ancient provinces of China, surely indistinguishable at this altitude.
But according to Tsou Yen (c. 300 B.C.) China is itself one of nine
continents each separated from the rest by impassible seas. Probably
the immortal who tries to make out China sees all nine inside the tiny
cupful of the ocean.

Up in Heaven

The River of Heaven turns in the night and floats the
stars round,
A stream of cloud between silver shores mimics the
sound of water.
The cassia tree of the Jade Palace has never shed its
flowers,
A houri plucks their fragrance to hang at her jewelled
sash.

The Ch'in princess rolls back the blind, day breaks at
the North window:
Before the window the straight *wu-t'ung* dwarfs the blue
phoenix.
The prince blows the long goose-quills of the pan-pipes,
Calling to the dragon to plough the mist and plant the
jasper herb.

With ribbons of pale dawn-cloud pink and lotus-root
fibre skirts
Fairies walk on Azure Isle gathering orchids in the
spring.
They point at Hsi-ho in the Eastern sky, who so deftly
speeds his horses,
While out of the sea the new land silts beneath the stony
mountains.

Hsi-ho: the charioteer of the sun.

A Bronze Immortal takes Leave of Han

In the eighth month of the first year of the Blue Dragon period
(A.D. 233) the Emperor Ming of Wei sent a court chamberlain
with carts to transport from the west the Emperor Wu of Han's
immortals bearing pans to catch the dew, wishing to set them up
in the front hall of his own palace. After the chamberlain had
split off the pans, just as the immortals were about to be loaded,
tears gushed from them. I, Li Ho of the Imperial house of
T'ang, have taken this as theme for my song of an immortal
taking leave of Han.

Boy Liu in Leafy Mound, visitor of the autumn wind ...
In the night I heard his horse whinny, at sunrise saw no
    track.
On the cassia tree by the painted rail the scent of autumn
    hangs:
In his thirty-six palaces the dust blooms emerald.

Wei's servants haul the cart, point ahead a thousand
    miles:
A sour wind shoots from the east pass at my pupils.
The moon of Han in vain with me I come forth at the
    palace gate:
At your memory the transparent tears are like molten
    lead.

Withering orchids escort me along the Hsien-yang
    road:
If heaven too had passions even heaven would grow
    old.
With the pan in my hands I come forth alone under the
    desolate moon:
The city on the Jwei far back now, quiet the waves.

The Emperor Wu (140–87 B.C.) of the Han dynasty (206 B.C.–A.D. 220) wrote a prose poem *Autumn Wind* (translated by Waley) which ends: 'Youth's years how few, age how sure!' Obsessed by the longing for immortality he set up pans held by bronze immortals to catch the dew for the elixir. The Emperor who sought immortality died and was buried at Mao-ling (Leafy Mound). Now the Han dynasty of his family the Liu has perished; the bronze statues remain, and remember him as 'Young Liu in Leafy Mound', who vanished as though in the autumn wind of his own writing, as swiftly as horses passing in the night. The opening stanza seems also to have a secondary suggestion of the statue hearing in the night wind its master's ghost returning to haunt his palaces where the moss-grown floors 'bloom emerald'.

The statues are at the Han capital Ch'ang-an in the north-west. There is a further allusion to the passing of dynasties in the last stanza, which mentions the nearby capital of the preceding Ch'in dynasty (221–207 B.C.) under both its Ch'in name of Hsien-yang and its Han name of Wei-ch'eng ('City on the Jwei'). The new Wei dynasty (A.D. 220–264) transports the statues to its new capital at Lo-yang beyond the East pass. The bronze immortal weeps because its lords the Han Emperors are dead, because it, too, has been drawn into the vicissitudes of the living, because in weeping its unchanging metal is moved by the passions which age men.

The moon, which suggests mutability to us, suggests permanence to the Chinese; the moon and the cassia tree which grows on it are among Li Ho's favourite symbols of escape from time (cf. *A Dream of Heaven*, *Up in Heaven*). It was to the moon that Ch'ang O fled after stealing the elixir of life (cf. Li Shang-yin's *Ch'ang O*, *Frosty Moon*); it is there, too, that the elixir is pounded by the hare (cf. *A Dream of Heaven*: Lu T'ung's *Eclipse* also mentions both the Lady of the Moon and the hare). References to the moon and the cassia recur in the third line of each stanza, with faint suggestions of immortality out of reach – the autumn scent of the earthly cassia, the 'moon of Han', the desolate moon.

There are two current explanations of the 'moon of Han', as the pan for the dew, and as the moon itself, which the statue vainly regards as still belonging to Han, because it is the only thing in the landscape which the Wei cannot steal. There seems to be no objection to accepting both, and even finding a connexion between them. The Han Emperor sought in the pans the elixir which is only on the moon; from one point of view he was claiming that his power extends to the moon, from another taking the pan as his moon. The parallels and contrasts between the third lines of the last two stanzas are suggestive;

in the former the statue is accompanied by the 'moon of Han', in the latter it is 'alone' with the pan and the 'desolate moon'.

The commentator Wang Ch'i writes (A.D. 1760):

'Ssŭ-ma Kuang (1019–86) notes in his poetry criticisms: "Li Ho's

'If heaven too had passions even heaven would grow old'

is a peerless line. Shih Yen-nien (994–1041) emulated it with

'If the moon knew no yearning the moon would be always round,'

which people think a close rival to it." I have maturely considered the two lines; they exhibit the whole difference between the natural and the forced; there is no comparison between them.'

High Dike

I am a woman of Heng-t'ang.
My crimson silks are full of the scent of cassia.
A black cloud binds up a topknot for my head,
The full moon shapes me a pearl for my ear.
> A breeze rises in the lotus.
> On the banks of the river, spring.
> Here on High Dike
> I stop the men from the north.
> You shall eat carp's tails,
> I shall eat monkey's lips.
Don't point towards Hsiang-yang,
By the green shores are few returning sails.
Today we blossom with the reeds,
Tomorrow with the maple grow old.

Dawn in Stone City

The moon has set above High Dike,
From their perch on the parapet crows fly up.
Fine dew damps the rounded crimson
And the cold scent clears of last night's drunkenness.
Woman and herdboy have crossed the River of Heaven,
Mist in the willows fills the corners of the wall.
The favoured guest snaps off his tassel for a pledge:
Two eyebrows, smudges of green, knit.

Spring curtains of flimsy cicada-wing gauze,
Spread cushions braided with gold, and a flower which
    hides away.
In front of the curtain light willow fluff hovers, crane's
    down –
No, for spring's passion there is no simile.

The King of Ch'in drinks Wine

The King of Ch'in rides out on his tiger and roams to
the Eight Bounds,
The flash of his sword lights up the sky against the
resisting blue:
He is Hsi-ho flogging the sun forward with the sound of
ringing glass.
The ashes of the kalpas have flown away, rebellion has
never been.
Dragon's heads spout wine and the Wine Star is his
guest,
Gold-grooved mandolins twang in the night;
The feet of the rain on Lake Tung-t'ing come blown on
a gust from the pan-pipes,
Heated by the wine his shout makes the moon run
backward!

Under combed layers of silvered cloud the jasper hall
brightens,
A messenger from the palace gate reports the first watch.
The jade phoenix of the painted tower has a sweet and
fierce voice,
Mermaid silks patterned in crimson have a faint and
cool scent.
The yellow swans trip over in the dance. A thousand
years in the cup!

Beneath the immortal's tree of candles, where the wax
lightly smokes,
The tears flood Blue Zither's drunken eyes.

The King of Ch'in is Shih-huang-ti, who unified China by the conquest of all rival states in 221 B.C. His glory, his search for the elixir of life, and the quick collapse of his Empire after his death, lie unstated in the background of this poem in which the drunken king imagines himself victor over time, driving the sun and calling back the moon. In his ecstasy he roams to the eight cardinal and intermediate points at the limits of the universe; he becomes Hsi-ho the charioteer of the sun; as though the preceding kalpas (Buddhist world-cycles) had never been, he begins history with his pacification of the world. As the poem proceeds images of power and luxury (silks woven by the 'Shark People' or mermaids, dancers in swan costumes) are shot through with suggestions that time is after all passing – moonlight brightening on the roof, the report of the watch, finally the concubine with the name of the nymph Blue Zither with tears in her eyes (of joy or sorrow?) under the candles gradually burning away in the candelabra held by a carved immortal.

The seventh line condenses into one image comparisons between the music and that played for the legendary Yellow Emperor on Lake Tung-t'ing, between raindrops and feet on water, between the notes of pan-pipes and raindrops on water, perhaps also between the tubes graduated from longer to shorter and rain slanting in wind.

The Grave of Little Su

I ride a coach with lacquered sides,
My love rides a dark piebald horse.
Where shall we bind our hearts as one?
On West Mound, beneath the pines and cypresses.
    (Ballad ascribed to the singing girl Little Su, *c.* A.D. 500)

Dew on the secret orchid
Like crying eyes.
No thing to bind the heart to.
Misted flowers I cannot bear to cut.
Grass like a cushion,
The pine like a parasol:
The wind is a skirt,
The waters are tinkling pendants.
A coach with lacquered sides
Waits for someone in the evening.
Cold blue candle-flames
Strain to shine bright.
Beneath West Mound
The wind puffs the rain.

From Criticisms
(Third of five)

The Southern hills, how mournful!
A ghostly rain sprinkles the empty grass.
In Ch'ang-an, on an autumn midnight,
How many men grow old before the wind?
Dim, dim, the path in the twilight,
Branches curl on the black oaks by the road.
The trees cast upright shadows and the moon at the
    zenith
Covers the hills with a white dawn.
Darkened torches welcome a new kinsman:
In the most secret tomb these fireflies swarm.

In the last couplet the will-o'-the-wisp is apparently welcoming Li Ho
into the land of the dead, as a bride is welcomed into her husband's
family.

A Girl Combs her Hair

Hsi-shih dreams at dawn, in the cool of silk curtains:
A tress has slipped from the scented knot over the fading
rouge.
The pulley creaks at the well, winds up with a jade
tinkle
And startles awake this lotus which has just slept its fill.
Two birds on the flaps disclose the mirror, an autumn
sunlit pool.
She loosens the knots and looks down in the mirror as
she stands on the ivory bed.

> The chignon's perfumed threads spread cloudy on
> the floor:
> Where the jade comb falls, lustre and no sound.
> Slender fingers coil back the rooky sheen
> With a glint of blue, too sleek to lodge the hairpin.
> Casual spring breezes vex her languid grace:
> After eighteen tiresome knots, all force spent.

Her toilet done, the dressed hair slants and does not sag.
She measures her steps in the cloudy skirt, as a goose
walks on sand;
Turns away, still without speaking. What has caught
her eye?
She goes down the steps and picks the cherry flowers.

The Watchman's Drum in the Streets of Officials

The sound of its thump at dawn hurries the circling sun,
The sound at eve hurries the moonrise.
The willows of the Han capital shine yellow on the new
blinds,
Flying Swallow's scented bones lie buried in the cypress
mound;
It has pounded to pieces a thousand years of suns for
ever white
Unheard by the King of Ch'in and Emperor Wu.
Your hair glints blue, is the colour of the blossoms on
the reeds:
Try if you can to stand fast in China alone beside South
Mountain!
Through how many funerals of the blessed in heaven
The clock's drip-drip sounds on without a pause!

'Colour of the blossoms on the reeds': white.

Don't Go Out of the Door

The Heavenly Questions *were written by Ch'ü Yüan (c. 300 B.C.).*
Why not call them 'Questions to Heaven'? Heaven is too august
to be questioned, so he called them 'Heavenly Questions'. Ch'ü
Yüan in exile, his anxious heart wasted with cares, roamed among
the mountains and marshes, crossed over the hills and plains, crying
aloud to the Most High, and sighing as he looked up at heaven. He
saw in Ch'u the shrines of the former kings and the ancestral halls of
the nobles, painted with pictures of heaven and earth, mountains and
rivers, gods and spirits, jewels and monsters, and the wonders and
the deeds of ancient sages. When he tired of wandering among them
he rested beneath them; and he took the pictures which he saw above
him as themes for writing on the walls his raving questions.

> (From the preface to the *Heavenly Questions* in the *Songs*
> *of Ch'ü*)

I plucked the autumn orchid to adorn my girdle.
> (Ch'ü Yüan, *Encountering Sorrows*)

Heaven is inscrutable,
Earth keeps its secrets.
The nine-headed monster eats our souls,
Frosts and snows snap our bones.
Dogs are set on us, snarl and sniff around us,
And lick their paws, partial to the orchid-girdled,
Till the end of all afflictions, when God sends us his
  chariot,
And the sword starred with jewels and the yoke of
  yellow gold.

I straddle my horse but there is no way back,
On the lake which swamped Li-yang the waves are huge
  as mountains,
Deadly dragons stare at me, jostle the rings on the
  bridle,

Lions and chimaeras spit from slavering mouths.
Pao Chiao slept all his life in the parted ferns,
Yen Hui before thirty was flecked at the temples,
Not that Yen Hui had weak blood
Nor that Pao Chiao had offended Heaven:
Heaven dreaded the time when teeth would close and
    rend them,
For this and this cause only made it so.
Plain though it is, I fear that still you doubt me.
Witness the man who raved at the wall as he wrote his
    questions to Heaven.

Musing
(First of two)

Ssŭ-ma Hsiang-ju pondered Leafy Mound
Where the green grasses drooped by the stone well,
Plucked his lute and gazed at Wen-chün,
And the spring breeze in her hair blew shadows on her
    temples.
The Prince of Liang, the Emperor Wu,
Had cast him off like a snapped stalk:
His only memorial, one writing on bamboo,
To be sealed in gold on the summit of Mount T'ai.

The poet Ssŭ-ma Hsiang-ju ran away with Wen-chün, daughter of
the rich man Cho Wang-sun. They settled by Leafy Mound (Mao-
ling), the tomb which the Emperor Wu (140–87 B.C.) had already
built for himself. When the poet was dying in 118 B.C. the Emperor
sent for his manuscripts, but none remained except a document for the
ceremonies on and under Mount T'ai, in which the Emperor reported
the achievements of his reign to Heaven and Earth.
    Li Ho is thinking of his own neglect, and of the comforts of a retired
life which only partly compensate for it.

Tu Mu (803–52)

Tu Mu is most admired as a master of the *chüeh-chü*, the New Style quatrain with an A A B A rhyme scheme like that of Omar Khayyam. The swift elegance of his verses, running effortlessly within strict formal limits, cannot be captured in my easy-going sprung rhythms. With his acutely sensual delight in wine, women, spring landscapes, and the brilliant colours of birds and flowers, he is a refreshing exception among the generally sombre poets of this volume. The times when he wandered putting up in the monasteries in Chiang-nan south of the Yangtse, favourite region of the Sung landscape painters, or rioting in the pleasure quarter of Yang-chou at the river's mouth, cost him some regrets; but there is more joy in him than in any T'ang poet later than Li Po.

Easing My Heart

By river and lakes at odds with life I journeyed, wine
    my freight:
Slim waists of Ch'u broke my heart, light bodies danced
    into my palm.
Ten years late I wake at last out of my Yang-chou
    dream
With nothing but the name of a drifter in the blue
    houses.

'Blue houses': brothels.

Egrets

Snowy coats and snowy crests and beaks of blue jade
Flock above the fish in the brook and dart at their own
   shadows,
In startled flight show up far back against the green hills,
The blossoms of a whole pear-tree shed by the evening
   wind.

Spring in Chiang-nan

For a thousand miles the oriole sings, crimson against
the green.
Riverside villages, mountain ramparts, wineshop
streamers in the wind.
Of four hundred and eighty monasteries of the Southern
Dynasties
How many towers and terraces loom in the misty rain?

To Judge Han Ch'o at Yang-chou

Over misted blue hills and distant water
In Chiang-nan at autumn's end the grass has not yet
    wilted.
By night on the Four-and-Twenty Bridges, under the
    full moon,
Where are you teaching a jade girl to blow tunes on your
    flute?

The Retired Official Yüan's High Pavilion

The West River's watershed sounds beyond the sky.
Shadows of pines in front of the studio sweep the clouds
    flat.
Who shall coax me to blow the long flute
Leaning together on the spring wind with the moon-
    beams for our toys?

The Gate Tower of Ch'i-an City

The sound grates on the river tower, one blast of the
    horn.
Pale sunlight floods, sinking by the cold shore.
Pointless to lean on the balcony and look back miserably:
There are seventy-five post-stations from here to home.

On the Road

Sadness at the hairs in the mirror is new no longer,
The stains on my coat are harder to brush away.
I waste my hopes by river and lakes, a fishing-rod in the
  hand
Which screens me from the Western sunlight as I look
  towards Ch'ang-an.

The Pool behind Ch'i-an

Pond-chestnuts poke through floating chickweed on the
    green brocade pool:
A thousand summer orioles sing as they play among
    the roses.
I watch the fine rain, alone all day,
While side by side the ducks and drakes bath in their
    crimson coats.

The mandarin duck, which never leaves its mate, is the symbol of
harmonious marriage.

Pien River blocked by Ice

For a thousand miles along the river, when the ice begins
    to close,
Harness jades and girdle jaspers tinkle at the jagged edge.
The drift of life's no different from the water under the
    ice
Hurrying Eastward day and night while no one notices.

At Clear Brook in Ch'ih-chou

Played with the brook, all day till twilight.
I count this autumn's white hairs, reflected to the roots.
What is it I have washed in you a thousand times over?
Of the clot on my brush-point, soon may there be no
    trace.

Travelling in the Mountains

Far up the cold mountain the stony path slopes:
Where the white clouds are born there are homes of men.
Stop the carriage, sit and enjoy the evening in the maple
    wood:
The frosty leaves are redder than the second month's
    flowers.

Farewell Poem
(Second of two to a girl of Yang-chou)

Passion too deep seems like none.
While we drink, nothing shows but the smile which will
    not come.
The wax candles feel, suffer at partings:
Their tears drip for us till the sky brightens.

In Ch'i-an, on a Chance Theme
(First of two)

The setting sun is two rods high on the bridge over the
brook,
Light floss of mist curls half way up from the shadows
of the willows.
So many green lotus-stalks lean on each other yearning!
... For an instant they turn their heads to the West
wind behind them.

The lotuses, like the poet, look towards the sunset and Ch'ang-an.

Shih Ch'ung's 'Golden Valley' Garden

. . . Just then Ch'ung was feasting on the top storey of his mansion.
'Now I shall be executed on account of you', he told Green Pearl.
She answered weeping: 'It is right that I should give my life in
your presence.' Then she threw herself from the top storey and was
killed.   (Biography of Shih Ch'ung (249–300))

Scattered pomp has fallen to the scented dust.
The streaming waters know no care, the weeds claim
    spring for their own.
In the East wind at sunset the plaintive birds cry:
Petals on the ground are her likeness still beneath the
    tower where she fell.

Recalling former Travels No. 1

Whirled ten years beyond all bounds,
Treating myself in the taverns, drinking my own health.
In autumn hills and spring rain in the places where I
　idly sang
I lolled against the pillars of every monastery in
　Chiang-nan.

Recalling former Travels No. 2

Caught in a storm outside Cloud Gate Abbey.
Against black woods on the high hill, long streaks of
　the rain.
Once at the Altar of Heaven I was acolyte. . . .
Glittering at attention, the Palace Guard's spears.

Recalling former Travels No. 3

Li Po put it in a poem, this West-of-the-Waters Abbey.
Old trees and crooked cliffs, wind in the upper rooms.
Between drunk and sober I drifted three days
While blossoms white and crimson opened in the misty
　rain.

Climbing to Lo-yu Plateau, before leaving for Wu-hsing

The flavour in mild times, there are no great men.
I love the lone cloud's idleness and the stillness of the
    monks.
Before I'm gone, banner in hand, to the river and the sea,
From the plain above the capital I'll look out on
    T'ai-tsung's tomb.

T'ai-tsung (627–49), second T'ang Emperor.

Autumn Evening

Silvery autumn candlelight chills the painted screen,
A little fan of light silk flaps the streaming fireflies.
Cool as water, the night sheen of the steps into the sky.
She lies and watches the Weaver Girl meet the Herdboy
    Star.

This poem has also been ascribed to Wang Chien (768?–830?). There
is disagreement as to whether the first and third lines refer to a candle
in the room and steps outside the window or to the moon and the 'Sky
Stair', six stars in Ursa Major.

  The Weaver Girl (Vega) and Herdboy (in Aquila) are stars parted
by the Milky Way; they meet once a year on the Seventh Night of the
Seventh Month (the first month of autumn).

Red Slope
(Last of three)

Milky in the spring grotto stone fattens, sprouts goose-
quills:
Rockpools veer with the crooked cliff along dog-
toothed edges.
I smile at myself, wound up in the bosom now; and,
with horns plucked in,
Spiral back up the misty steps like a snail.

This is one of three nostalgic poems about Red Slope at Fan-ch'uan,
Tu Mu's childhood home, to which he returned just before his death.
Tu Mu imagines himself, after he retires from office, withdrawing into
the winding passages of the cave like a snail shrinking into its shell.

Most of the imagery is rooted in ordinary Chinese idiom. Slender
hollow stalactites were called 'goose-quill stones'; irregular edges
fitting together like a dog's teeth were called 'dog-toothed' (cf.
English 'dovetailed'). The snail for the Chinese is a humble creature,
but without its slimy associations for a nation of gardeners suspicious
of French cooking; 'sticking out the horns' was a common idiom for
entering public life, and 'snail's shell' for the home of a man retiring
into privacy.

The phrase 'wound up in the bosom' is from the *Analects of Con-
fucius* (15/7), where, according to the interpretation which Tu Mu
seems to be following, Confucius says of a certain minister that 'when
the country was rightly governed, he took office; when it was not, he
let himself be wound up and slipped into the bosom' (like an article
wrapped and put away until needed again). It is a metaphor for retire-
ment from office, but also points forward to the image of the snail
coiled inside its shell. Readers impressed by the Freudian look of the
first line (dripping teats? the womb?) will also be reminded of the
mother's breast.

Li Shang-yin (812?–58)

It is well known that the theme of love has a much smaller place in Chinese poetry than in our own. Tenderness in classical poetry, however deep, is a temperate feeling for friends, kinsmen and – in no different spirit – wives; any more violent passion is an excess unsuitable for poetry; the only physical intoxication which offers glimpses of eternity is the ecstasy of wine. This mistrust of violence and cultivation of serenity is easily mistaken for weakness of feeling; but it might be better to take it as a sign that desire has not yet deteriorated to the point, reached in Europe less than two centuries ago, at which the ancient fear of being overthrown by the passions begins to be exchanged for the modern worry about dying of emotional atrophy. In any case, the gentlemanly reserve of the Chinese, like the impassiveness of the English, is very much a matter of class. We do find the theme of love in the most ancient collection of all, the *Book of Songs* (c. 800–600 B.C.), and it reappears in the folk poetry of the fourth century A.D., in the song lyrics (*tʒ'ŭ*) of the late T'ang and the Sung (960–1279), and in the drama and novel, long despised as vulgar, which are the true literature of China from the Yüan (1280–1367) onwards. It has also inspired a genre peculiar to China, the memoir of a dead wife or concubine to which Lin Yutang has called attention, of which the *Six Chapters of a Floating Life* of Shen Fu (1763–?), translated in Lin Yutang's *Wisdom of China*, contains what is perhaps the most beautiful example.

Even the generalization that classical poetry takes no notice of love is true only with qualifications, and in the ninth century it is hardly true at all. From about 800 poetry began to move indoors, in particular behind the doors of courtesans, from which the *tʒ'ŭ* was emerging. Nature is seen increasingly in terms of the artificial; Tu Mu's ducks wear crimson coats, his pool is covered with a brocade of chickweed, he hears the crackle of forming ice as the tinkle of jade. In some poems of Li Ho there is already a foretaste of the feminine, silken, flower-decked, phoenix-infested imagery of the ninth century, glittering with pearls and jades, heavily scented with cassia or incense, dripping with the tears of wax candles. Women are at the centre of this sumptuousness, if only as the most luxurious article of all; and the love of women is the major theme of the one great poet of the period, Li Shang-yin.

Until very recently commentators were embarrassed by this awkward fact, and explained many of his poems as political allegories or as threnodies for his wife, advised the reader to respect the poet's privacy in others, dismissed a few as licentious. Their discomfort can be understood even without allowing for the assumption that love is an un-poetical theme; for it seems obvious that many poems, especially among those which carry the title 'Untitled', reflect a secret, desperate, and apparently guilty love quite different from the usual undemanding affairs with singing girls. One untranslated poem, The Refining of the Elixir (Yao chuan), seems to describe a secret abortion; at any rate, the commentator Feng Hao (1719–1801) understood it in this sense, much to his distaste, and he suspected the same significance, perhaps unjustly, in the last verse of the mysterious Walls of Emerald. Li Shang-yin's poems excite the same kind of extra-literary curiosity as Shakespeare's sonnets, although even in the present century Su Hsüeh-lin is almost the only critic to discuss such questions publicly.

A few of the poem titles mention women by name, Liu Chih ('Willow Branch') and the Taoist nun Sung of Hua-yang nunnery. Willow is very probably addressed to the former, and we may recognize the latter in the woman compared in several poems with Ch'ang O, who fled from earth to the cold solitude of the moon after stealing the elixir of life. (Many Taoist nuns of the T'ang dynasty were daughters or concubines of the Emperor or of high officials, put away by their lords or voluntarily resorting to this permitted refuge; some used their education and high connexions to live as high-class courtesans. The Taoist pursuit of immortality was, in any case, a rather different matter from the contemplative life in the Christian West, and there would be no flavour of sacrilege about the episode.) As for the girl in some of the *Untitled Poems*, Su Hsüeh-lin thinks that she was an Imperial concubine, but this seems too romantic to be easily believable. More plausible is the older suggestion that she was a concubine of Li Shang-yin's second political patron Wang Mao-yüan, whose daughter he married in 838. *First Month: at Ch'ung-jang House* supports this suggestion; Ch'ung-jang House was Wang Mao-yüan's residence at Loyang. The romantic value of love for Li Shang-yin shows startlingly in certain poems about Imperial concubines, *Crooked River* and *Ma-wei*, which assume, to the disgust of commentators, that a private love should matter more to an Emperor than the ruin of his state.

Li Shang-yin, unlike Li Ho, is among the stable reputations in T'ang poetry. The metaphorical complexity of his couplets, in which one scarcely ever meets a simile, will be examined in detail in the notes to several of his poems. His use of allusion is the subtlest in T'ang poetry – abrupt transitions in which an allusion provides the unmentioned bridge, delicate variations on commonplace references, oblique glimpses of historical events, direct presentation of a scene before his eyes in which one senses elusive parallels with a scene in history or poetry. But in spite of ambiguous wordplay which cannot be transferred to another language, and allusions which it is often profitless to explain, it should be possible, whether or not I succeed myself, to translate him very effectively – much more effectively than Tu Fu, an unquestionably greater poet who may seem his inferior in English, because Tu Fu's imagery does not reach as far into our instinctive depths as imagery with erotic roots. Li Shang-yin's language has a vitality independent of the allusions which enrich it:

VAST SEA MOON FULL / PEARL HAVE TEAR

The line, from *The Patterned Lute*, is not fully intelligible without knowledge of two allusions which establish the connexion between the moonlit sea and the tears on the pearl. But even before recognizing them, 'moon' is already interacting in one's imagination with 'pearl', 'pearl' with 'sea', 'sea' with 'tear'.

Untitled Poems

(The untitled poems are scattered over Li Shang-yin's collected verse; the present selection is numbered only for convenience.)

(i)

Coming was an empty promise, you have gone, and left
    no footprint:
The moonlight slants above the roof, already the fifth
    watch sounds.
Dreams of remote partings, cries which cannot summon,
Hurrying to finish the letter, ink which will not thicken.
The light of the candle half encloses kingfishers threaded
    with gold,
The smell of musk comes faintly through embroidered
    water-lilies.
      Young Liu complained that Fairy Hill is far.
Past Fairy Hill, range above range, ten thousand
    mountains rise.

'Fairy Hill': P'eng-lai, one of the mountains of the immortals in
the Eastern sea. 'Young Liu' is a slightly contemptuous reference to
the Emperor Wu of Han's search for immortality, as in Li Ho's *Bronze
Immortal*.

(ii)

The East wind sighs, the fine rains come:
Beyond the pool of water-lilies, the noise of faint
    thunder.
A gold toad gnaws the lock. Open it, burn the incense.
A tiger of jade pulls the rope. Draw from the well and
    escape.
Chia's daughter peeped through the screen when Han
    the clerk was young,
The goddess of the river left her pillow for the great
    Prince of Wei.
Never let your heart open with the spring flowers:
One inch of love is an inch of ashes.

Thoughts are in a hollow space in the heart one inch square (cf. Meng
Chiao's *Wanderer's Song*). The last line also suggests two of Li Shang-
yin's favourite images of love, a continuing thread and a candle flame
(cf. for example the second couplet of the sixth *Untitled Poem*).

(iii)
Bite back passion. Spring now sets.
Watch little by little the night turn round.
Echoes in the house; want to go up, dare not.
A glow behind the screen; wish to go through, cannot.
It would hurt too much, the swallow on a hairpin;
Truly shame me, the phoenix on a mirror.
    On the road back, sunrise over Heng-t'ang.
The blossoming of the morning-star shines farewell on
    the jewelled saddle.

Heng-t'ang was a pleasure quarter; cf. Li Ho's *High Dike*.

(iv)

Last night's stars, last night's winds,

By the West wall of the painted house, East of the hall
of cassia.

For bodies no fluttering side by side of splendid phoenix
wings,

For hearts the one minute thread from root to tip of the
magic horn.

At separate tables, played hook-in-the-palm. The wine
of spring warmed.

Teamed as rivals, guessed what the cup hid. The candle
flame reddened.

Alas, I hear the drum, must go where office summons,

Ride my horse to the Orchid Terrace, the wind-
uprooted weed my likeness.

The white core of the unicorn's horn was treasured (as an
Aphrodisiac?).
    'Orchid Terrace': a secretariat at the capital.

(v)

Phoenix tail on scented silk, flimsy layer on layer:

Blue patterns on a round canopy, stitched deep into the
  night.

The fan's sliced moon could not hide her shame,

His coach drove out with the sound of thunder, no time
  to exchange a word.

In the silent room the gold of the wick turned dark:

No message since has ever come, though the pome-
  granate is red.

The dappled horse stands tethered only on the bank of
  drooping willows,

Where shall she wait for a kind wind to blow from the
  South West?

Red pomegranate wine is drunk on the wedding night. The girl is
apparently stitching the canopy of her bridal bed; the man has aban-
doned her to 'pluck the willow at Chang Terrace' (visit a prostitute).
There is a detailed analysis of this poem and the next in James Liu's
Art of Chinese Poetry (London, 1962), 137–41.

(vi)
For ever hard to meet, and as hard to part.
Each flower spoils in the failing East wind.
Spring's silkworms wind till death their heart's threads:
The wick of the candle turns to ash before its tears dry.
Morning mirror's only care, a change at her cloudy
    temples:
Saying over a poem in the night, does she sense the
    chill in the moonbeams?
      Not far, from here to Fairy Hill.
Bluebird, be quick now, spy me out the road.

(vii)

Where is it, the sad lyre which follows the quick flute?
Down endless lanes where the cherries flower, on a bank
    where the willows droop.
The lady of the East house grows old without a husband,
The white sun at high noon, the last spring month half
    over.
        Princess Li-yang is fourteen,
In the cool of the day, after the Rain Feast, with him
    behind the fence, look.
. . . Come home, toss and turn till the fifth watch.
Two swallows in the rafters hear the long sigh.

(viii)

'... *Just before dawn she left. She gave Wen-shao a gold hairpin, and he gave her a silver bowl and a porcelain spoon. Next day he came across them in the Blue Brook shrine; and then he understood that the girl whom he had met was the goddess of Blue Brook.*'

> '*Where the door opens on the white water*
> *A little way from the bridge,*
> *That's the house of the little maid*
> *Who lives alone without a lover.*'
>   (The Girl of Blue Brook)

Double curtains hang deep in the room of Never Grieve:
She lies down, and moment by moment the cool evening
    lengthens.
The lifetime he shared with the goddess was always a
    dream:
No young man ever in the little maid's house.
The wind and waves know no pity for the frail pond-
    chestnut's branches,
In the moon and the dew who can sweeten the scentless
    cassia leaves?
        We tell ourselves all love is foolishness ——
And still disappointment is a lucid madness.

Never Grieve (Mo-ch'ou) appears in *The Water of the River* by the Emperor Wu of Liang (502–49), as the dissatisfied wife of the rich Lu. T'ang poets liked her for the irony of her name, and Li Shang-yin no doubt also for the relevance to his own case of the last couplet:
'So rich and honoured, what is there left to wish for?
She pines that she missed being married to her next-door neighbour
    Wang.'
Li Shang-yin's second couplet, which seems to imply a brief love-meeting remembered as though it were a dream, exploits the odd contrast between the popular quatrain about the girl of Blue Brook and the story of her as an amorous nymph, like the goddess of Mount Wu who visited King Huai in a dream (cf. *Peonies*).

Li Shang-yin's third couplet no doubt describes the moonlit pool and cassia tree outside his window, but also hints at a comparison of the girl with the unreachable Ch'ang O by the cassia tree on the moon (cf. *Ch'ang O, Frosty Moon* and perhaps the sixth line of the sixth *Untitled Poem*).

Willow

('Willow eyebrows' is a phrase used for both willow leaves and arched eyebrows.)

Boundless the leaves roused by spring,
Countless the twigs which tremble in the dawn.
Whether the willow can love or not,
Never a time when it does not dance.
Blown fluff hides white butterflies,
Drooping bands disclose the yellow oriole.
The beauty which shakes a kingdom must reach through
    all the body:
Who comes only to view the willow's eyebrows?

The Lady in the Moon

'Ch'ang O Stole the herb of immortality and fled to the moon.
Because the moon is white, she is called the White Beauty.'
'In the third autumn month, the Dark Maid emerges to send
down the frost and snow' (cf. Tu Fu, *The Autumn Wastes*, No. 4).

(i) Ch'ang O

The lamp glows deep in the mica screen.
The long river slowly descends, the morning star
    drowns.
Is Ch'ang O sorry that she stole the magic herb,
Between the blue sky and the emerald sea, thinking
    night after night?

(ii) Frosty Moon

First calls of the migrant geese, no more cicadas.
South of this hundred-foot tower the water runs straight
    to the sky.
The Dark Maid and the White Beauty endure the cold
    together,
Rivals in elegance amid the frost on the moon.

Exile

A spring day at the edge of the world.
On the edge of the world once more the day slants.
The oriole cries, as though it were its own tears
Which damp even the topmost blossoms on the tree.

'Day' and 'sun' are one word in Chinese, as are 'moon' and 'month'.
Cf. the title of *Frosty Moon*, and the last couplet but one of Han Yü's
Autumn Thoughts. The 'edge of the world' is also punned. There is
no other 'as though' or 'like' in the here translated poetry of Li Shang-
yin, who generally avoids explicit simile.

First Month: at Ch'ung-jang House

Secret behind locks and double bars, covered with green
moss.
In the deepest corridors, innermost chambers, pacing to
and fro.
A presage that the wind will rise – the halo round the
moon.
The season of cold dews still, the buds unopened.
A bat sweeps past the flap of the blind. Endless tossing
and turning.
A mouse unsettles the cobweb on the window, startles
with brief suspicions.
With the lamp at my back I talk alone to a fragrance still
in the air,
And unawares, just as before, sing *Rise in the Night and
Come.*

Day after Day

Day after day spring's glory vies with the glorious sun.
Sloping roads to the hill city smell of flowering almond.
How long before the heart's threads, all cares gone,
Float free for a hundred feet with the gossamer?

Night Rains: to my Wife up North

You ask how long before I come. Still no date is set.
The night rains on Mount Pa swell the autumn pool.
When shall we, side by side, trim a candle at the West
    window,
And talk back to the time of the night rains on Mount
    Pa?

To Tzŭ-chih: among the 'Flowers'

The light on the pool suddenly hides behind the wall,
Mingled scents of flowers invade the room.
On the edge of the screen, powder smeared by the
    butterfly:
On the lacquered window the yellow print of the bee.
Push those state papers across to the clerks,
There's a maid for every honest civil servant.
Let's ride abreast and hear each other's poems.
What's so urgent about this business you waste your
    heart on?

Written on a Monastery Wall

They rejected life to seek the Way. Their footprints are
    before us.
They offered up their brains, ripped up their bodies; so
    firm was their resolution.
See it as large, and a millet-grain cheats us of the
    universe:
See it as small, and the world can hide in a pinpoint.
The oyster before its womb fills thinks of the new
    cassia;
The amber, when it first sets, remembers a former pine.
If we trust the true and sure words written on Indian
    leaves
We hear all past and future in one stroke of the temple
    bell.

The fifth line refers to the cassia tree on the moon. The pearl grows
inside the oyster with the waxing of the moon (cf. *Patterned Lute*).

Crooked River

Lost in the distance, the peaceful time when the green
    palanquin passed:
Vain to listen to the lovesong which a ghost sadly sings.
The golden car no more brings back the beauty which
    spoiled cities
Where the hall of jade still cleaves the ripples in the
    lower park.
. . . dying remembered Hua-t'ing, heard the whoop of
    cranes . . .
. . . grown old, fearful for a royal house, wept by the
    bronze camels . . .
Heaven desolate and earth in discord, but though his
    heart broke,
His wound was lighter than the pain of spring.

The Emperor Wen-tsung (809–40) used to take his concubine Yang
Hsien-fei to Crooked River Park South of Ch'ang-an. The park fell
into neglect after the Kan-lu rebellion (835), and Yang Hsien-fei was
executed immediately after the Emperor's death, events to which the
last couplet seems to allude.

As images of civil disorder, the third couplet gives fragmentary
oblique glimpses of older revolutions:

'When Lu Chi (261–303) was seized, he sighed: "Shall I ever again
hear the cranes call at Hua-t'ing?"'

'So Ching (239–303) knowing that rebellion was imminent pointed
at the bronze camels by Lo-yang palace gate and sighed: "The time is
coming when we shall see you covered with brambles."'

                          (*History of the Chin dynasty*)

Ma-wei

The Emperor commanded a magician to bring back the ghost of Yang Kuei-fei. The magician went east to the ends of the Sea of Heaven, crossed over P'eng-hu, and saw on the highest mountain many tall houses and watch-towers. On the West side he found an avenue of doors and a sign saying: 'The House of Yang Kuei-fei' ...

Just before leaving the magician asked Yang Kuei-fei to tell him of some incident known only to the Emperor and herself, which he might use as proof that he had met her. She stepped back and stood with an abstracted expression as though she were thinking of something. At last she said: 'In the tenth year of T'ien-pao (751) I was attending His Majesty at the summer palace on Black Horse Mountain. On the night of the meeting of the Herdboy and Weaver-girl stars (the Seventh of the Seventh Month), just on midnight, he dismissed the attendants and guards to the east and west wings, and I alone waited on His Majesty. Then he looked up at the sky, moved by the tale of the Herdboy and the Weaver-girl, and we secretly swore to each other to be husband and wife through all future lives. After he had spoken, he grasped my hand and each of us choked with tears. This is something that no one but my lord the Emperor knows.'

When the magician returned to report, the Emperor was stunned by grief.

(From the story of Yang Kuei-fei, concubine of the Emperor Ming-huang (713–55). The Emperor, fleeing from the rebel An Lu-shan, was forced to execute her at Ma-wei by his own mutinous troops, who resented the power of the Yang family.)

An empty rumour, that second world beyond the seas.
Other lives we cannot divine, this life is finished.

In vain she hears the Tiger Guards sound the night
   rattle,
Never again shall the Cock Man come to report the
   sunrise.
This is the day when six armies conspire to halt their
   horses:
The Seventh Night of another year mocked the Herdboy
   Star.
What matter that for four decades he was Son of
   Heaven?
He is less than Lu who married Never Grieve.

Peonies

Translation

The brocade curtains have just rolled back. Behold the
    Queen of Wei.

Still he piles up the embroidered quilts, Prince O in
    Yüeh.

Drooping hands disturb, tip over, pendants of carved
    jade:

Snapping waists compete in the dance, fluttering saffron
    skirts.

Shih Ch'ung's candles – but who would clip them?

Hsün Yü's braziers, where no incense fumes.

I who was given in a dream the brush of many colours

Wish to write on petals a message to the clouds of
    morning.

Paraphrase

The peonies have just burst their buds, like the Queen of
Wei rolling back the brocade curtain behind which she
received Confucius. New leaves still grow above the flowers
like the embroidered quilts which Prince O piled over his
lover in the boat when he visited Yüeh.

In a light breeze the flowers dip like the sleeves of girls in
the slow dance Drooping Hands, upsetting dewdrops like
the carved white-jade pendants on the dancers' girdles. In a
strong wind, the stalks bend double like girls in the fast
dance Snapping Waists, fluttering petals like saffron skirts.

The peonies blaze like the massed candles on which the
epicure Shih Ch'ung cooked his banquet. But their splendour
is natural; candles burn only if their wicks are trimmed, and
it would be intolerable to cut the peonies. They exhale

fragrance like censers; but their scent is natural like the perfume of Hsün Yü's body, which lingered for three days wherever he sat down.

The poet Chiang Yen dreamed that Kuo P'u's ghost came to recover his writing-brush of many colours; Chiang Yen returned it, and woke to find that he had lost his genius. The goddess of Mount Wu gave herself to King Huai in a dream and told him: 'At dawn I am the clouds of morning, at sunset the driving rain.' I, who dream that I possess the gift of poetry which Chiang Yen dreamed of losing, send you this letter, figuring your beauty in the beauty of the peony, and asking you to favour me as the goddess favoured King Huai.

The Walls of Emerald

1

Twelve turns of the rail on walls of emerald:
A sea-beast's horn repels the dust, a jade repels the cold.
Letters from Mount Lang-yüan have cranes for messengers,
On Lady's Couch a hen-phoenix perches in every tree.
The stars which sank to the bottom of the sea show up at the window:
The rain has passed where the River rises, far off you sit watching.
If the pearl of dawn should shine and never leave its place,
All life long we shall gaze in the crystal dish.

2

To glimpse her shadow, to hear her voice, is to love her.
On the pool of jade the lotus leaves spread out across the water.
Unless you meet Hsiao Shih with his flute, do not turn your head:
Do not look on Hung Ya, nor ever touch his shoulder.
The purple phoenix strikes a pose with the pendant of Ch'u in its beak:
The crimson scales dance wildly to the plucked strings on the river.
Prince O despairs of his night on the boat,
And sleeps alone by the lighted censer beneath the embroidered quilts.

3

On the Seventh Night she came at the time appointed.

The bamboo screens of the inner chamber have never since lifted.

On the jade wheel where the hare watches the dark begins to grow,

The coral in the iron net has still to put forth branches.

I have studied magic, can halt the retreat of day:

I have fetched phoenix papers and written down my love.

The Tale of the Emperor Wu is a plain witness:

Never doubt that the world of men can share this knowledge.

The Walls of Emerald is as obscure in Chinese as in English; it may well be that Li Shang-yin did not even wish to be understood except by the woman to whom he addressed it (his Taoist nun?). *The Tale of the Emperor Wu* records how the Western Queen Mother descended from the sky on the Seventh Night of the Seventh Month to teach the Emperor the science of immortality; it is hardly worth while to explain the other recognizable allusions. In Chinese the poem is an extraordinary example of a constellation of images which holds its irrational spell a thousand years after its meaning has been lost; readers may judge for themselves whether or not it survives the further transplantation to another language and culture.

The Patterned Lute

The Background of the Poem

Fu-hsi ordered the White Lady to strum the fifty-string lute. Because it was too sad, he forbade her to play, but she would not stop; so he broke her lute and left twenty-five strings.

Once Chuang-tʒŭ dreamed that he was a butterfly. . . . He does not know whether he is Chuang-tʒŭ who dreamed that he was a butterfly or a butterfly dreaming that he is Chuang-tʒŭ.

Wang-ti sent Pieh Ling to deal with the floods, and debauched his wife. He was ashamed, and considering Pieh Ling a better man than himself abdicated the state to him. At the time when Wang-ti left, the nightjar began to call. That is why the nightjar's call is sad to the people of Shu and reminds them of Wang-ti.

When Wang-ti died his soul turned into a bird called the 'nightjar'.

Po Ya strummed his lute, with his mind on climbing high mountains; and Chung Tʒŭ-ch'i said: 'Good! Lofty, like Mount T'ai!' When his mind was on flowing waters, Chung Tʒŭ-ch'i said: 'Good! Boundless like the Yellow River and the Yang-tse!'

When the moon is full the oyster has pearls, when the moon is dark the oyster is empty.

Beyond the South Sea there are mermaids ('shark people') who live in the water like fish, but spin like women on land; their weeping eyes can exude pearls.

When the King was dressing and combing himself, suddenly he saw Purple Jade. 'How can it be that you are alive?' he asked in his amaʒement, sad and happy at once. Purple Jade kneeled and said: 'Once young Han Chung came to seek me in marriage, and Your Majesty would not allow it; I lost my good name and atoned for it

169

by my death. . . .' Her mother heard them and came out to embrace her, but Purple Jade dissolved like smoke.

Tai Hsü-lun (732–89) said that the scene presented by a poet is like the smoke which issues from fine jade when the sun is warm on Blue Mountain (Lan-t'ien, ' Indigo Field'); it can be seen from a distance but not from close to.

Translation
Mere chance that the patterned lute has fifty strings.
String and fret, one by one, recall the blossoming years.
Chuang-tzŭ dreams at sunrise that a butterfly lost its
　　way,
Wang-ti bequeathed his spring passion to the nightjar.
The moon is full on the vast sea, a tear on the pearl.
On Blue Mountain the sun warms, a smoke issues from
　　the jade.
　　Did it wait, this mood, to mature with hindsight?
In a trance from the beginning, then as now.

Commentary

The *Patterned Lute* has long been famous as the most haunting and the most puzzling of Li Shang-yin's poems. The commentators Chu Hao-ling (1606–83) and Feng Hao (1719–1801) dismissed older stories that it recalls a nobleman's concubine or a maidservant of the poet's first political patron Ling-hu Ch'u, and insisted that it is a lament for his wife. 'A patterned lute longer than her' is in fact mentioned in a lament for his wife, the untranslated *Fang-chung ch'ü* (*Song inside the house*). But although this is still the most popular explanation, the reference to the adulterous love of Wang-ti points strongly to the dangerous intrigue of the *Untitled Poems*. These notes are offered with the warning that this dense poem has as many readings as readers.

Lines 1, 2. The fifty strings suggest a woman playing sadly like Fu-hsi's White Lady; playing them, the poet recalls an experience of his youth; the number also suggests a private chronological reference which has never been convincingly explained.

Lines 3, 4. The memory is of an adulterous love like Wang-ti's; like Chuang-tzǔ's dream it sometimes seems unreal, sometimes more real than the rest of life; like the nightjar which was once Wang-ti, the poet, changed for the worse by time, sings of a love which he remembers as though it happened to a different person.

'Chuang-tzǔ dreams *at sunrise* that a butterfly lost its way' raises the possibility that it was in waking from sleep that Chuang-tzǔ began to dream; it also allows one to take, not the dreamer, but the woman of whom he dreams, as the lost butterfly.

Lines 5, 6. As he plays, the music evokes the picture of a moonlit sea; the moon suggests a pearl in a sea of tears, pearls growing in the oyster with the waxing of the moon, mermaids who weep pearls, the girl who is moon, mermaid, and pearl. Then it conjures up Mount Lan-t'ien in the mist which is the smoke of its jade warmed by the sun, Purple Jade who died when she lost her lover and who dissolved like smoke when her mother tried to embrace her ghost, finally the girl who dissolves when the poet tries to fix her in his memory, whom he sees like a pearl behind a moist film or a precious stone through mist.

The striking parallel with Tai Hsü-lun's aphorism about poetry is often dismissed as a coincidence. If we accept its relevance, the couplet has another dimension. Maturing through time, like pearls forming as the moon waxes, painful experience becomes poetry, which crystallizes out of grief like a pearl from a tear, and depends for its beauty on distance, like the mountain mist.

Lines 7, 8. Is it only in memory that the experience has turned into a dream? Even at the time, it was lived as though in a trance.

When Yüan Hao-wen (1190–1257) made fun of the elaborate Hsi-k'un style inspired by Li Shang-yin, saying that it made contemporary poetry as unreadable without a commentary as the ancient *Book of Songs*, he used the *Patterned Lute* as his example:

'Wang-ti bequeathed his spring passion to the nightjar',
The girl's patterned lute laments the blossoming years.
All the poets love the Hsi-k'un style:
A pity that there's no Cheng Hsüan to write the commentary!

References

References are to the paging in the *Ch'üan T'ang shih* [Complete T'ang Poems], Peking, 1960.)

Tu Fu

41	2499
44	2475
45	2525
46	2560
47	2541
48	2523
49	2524
51	2509

Meng Chiao

59	4274
60	4210
61	4219
62	4226
63	4179
64	4179
65	4210
66	4184
67	4192
68	4206
69	4262

Han Yü

73	3767
74	3858
75	3832
76	3763

Lu T'ung

83	4364

Li Ho

93	4429
94	4434
95	4433
96	4403
97	4432
98	4429
99	4432
100	4399
102	4434
103	4399
104	4396
105	4399
106	4403
109	4395
110	4421
111	4400
113	4396
114	4411
115	4434
116	4435
117	4429
119	4394

Tu Mu

123	5998
124	5973
125	5964
126	5982
127	5983
128	5966
129	5985
130	5966
131	5983

Tu Mu

132	5967
133	5999
134	5988
135	5966
136	6013
137	5953
138	5961
139	6002
140	5959

Li Shang-yin

145	6163
146	6163
147	6164
148	6163
149	6202
150	6168
151	6164
152	6203
154	6150
155	6197
	6146
156	6193
157	6222
158	6195
159	6151
160	6211
161	6145
162	6224
163	6177
165	6171
167	6169
169	6144